'Call me,' Orlando said, his voice soft, and raised her hand to his mouth.

The brush of his lips against her skin was momentary. It was a mere courtesy, Eleanor knew—the Italian way of doing things. It didn't mean anything. But there was heat in his eyes. Heat matched by the flicker of desire rising up her spine.

Calling him would be way too dangerous for her peace of mind. But she wasn't going to argue over it now. Instead she smiled politely.

'Thank you for the lift, Dottore de Luca.'

'Orlando,' he corrected. *'Prego.'* He smiled, sketched a bow, ran lightly down the steps to his car and drove off…

MEDITERRANEAN DOCTORS

**Let these exotic doctors
sweep you off your feet…**

**Be tantalised by their smouldering
good-looks, romanced by their fiery
passion, and warmed by the emotional
power of these strong and caring men…**

MEDITERRANEAN DOCTORS
Passionate about life, love and medicine.

THE ITALIAN GP's BRIDE

BY
KATE HARDY

MILLS & BOON®
Pure reading pleasure

First published in Great Britain 2007
Large Print edition 2008
Harlequin Mills & Boon Limited,
Eton House, 18-24 Paradise Road,
Richmond, Surrey TW9 1SR

© Pamela Brooks 2007

ISBN: 978 0 263 19932 1

Set in Times Roman 16½ (
17-0208-52909

Printed and bound in Grea. _____
by Antony Rowe Ltd, Chippenham, Wiltshire

Kate Hardy lives in Norwich, in the east of England, with her husband, two young children, one bouncy spaniel, and too many books to count! When she's not busy writing romance or researching local history, she helps out at her children's schools; she's a school governor and chair of the PTA. She also loves cooking—see if you can spot the recipes sneaked into her books! (They're also on her website, along with extracts and stories behind the books.)

Writing for Harlequin Mills & Boon has been a dream come true for Kate—something she wanted to do ever since she was twelve. She's been writing Medical™ Romance for nearly five years now, and also writes for the Modern™ Extra series. She says it's the best of both worlds, because she gets to learn lots of new things when she's researching the background to a book: add a touch of passion, drama and danger, a new gorgeous hero every time, and it's the perfect job!

Kate's always delighted to hear from readers, so do drop in to her website at www.katehardy.com

Recent titles by the same author:

THE CONSULTANT'S NEW-FOUND FAMILY
IN THE GARDENER'S BED*
THEIR CHRISTMAS WISH
SEEING STARS*
THE FIREFIGHTER'S FIANCÉ
STRICTLY LEGAL*
Mills & Boon® Modern Extra

For Fi, with much love
(and thanks for the asparagus!)

CHAPTER ONE

'IF THERE'S a doctor on the plane, please could you make yourself known to the flight attendants by switching on the light above your head.'

The announcement that every doctor secretly dreaded. Especially on a plane, where space was so tight that it was difficult to work. Eleanor knew that the crew were trained in basic life support, so the problem was obviously something more complicated than that. They needed her help—her knowledge, her experience in emergency medicine. She switched on her light, and one of the flight attendants came over to her.

'One of our passengers has collapsed. Would you be able to take a look at her, please?' she asked in a low voice.

'Of course,' Eleanor said, keeping her voice equally low. She knew some people wouldn't want to get involved, but she'd never stand by and leave someone needing medical help. And in a way this was going to help her, too: instead of spending the whole of the flight from London to Naples wondering just what she was letting herself in for and worrying that maybe she wasn't doing the right thing, she had something to keep her mind occupied.

'Oh—do you have any identification?' The flight attendant swallowed hard. 'Sorry, I should've asked you that first.'

'No problem,' Eleanor said. Either the flight attendant was new to the job, or the emergency was something that had thrown her. Eleanor really hoped it was the former. The cramped aisle of an aeroplane, several thousand feet up in the air and half an hour from an ambulance wasn't the ideal place to deal with something major. 'You need proof that I'm a qualified doctor.' Luckily she kept her hospital ID card in her credit-card holder. She fished it out and showed it to the flight attendant, who looked relieved.

'Would you come this way, please, Dr Forrest? One of my colleagues is fetching the emergency kit.'

Eleanor followed her up the aisle to where a

middle-aged, plump woman was slumped in her seat. A quick check told her that the patient wasn't breathing and didn't have a pulse. She needed to get the woman flat and start CPR *now.*

'Did she bang her head at all?' she asked the woman seated next to her patient, who was sobbing.

The answer was a flow of Italian that Eleanor really couldn't follow.

Ah, hell. The chances were that the patient hadn't hit her head so there wasn't a risk of a spinal injury, and right now the most important thing was resuscitation. Just as she was about to ask the flight attendant to find someone who could speak Italian *and* English, to translate for her and get some help in moving the woman so Eleanor could start giving CPR, a man made his way down the aisle, following another flight attendant.

'Orlando de Luca, family doctor,' he introduced himself. 'May I help?'

His English was perfect, not halting in the slightest, though she was aware of his Italian accent. And he had the most beautiful mouth she'd ever seen.

Though now was absolutely *not* the time to be

thinking about that. They had a patient to save.
And right now she needed his skills—language
as well as medical. 'Eleanor Forrest, emergency
registrar,' she replied. 'Thank you. Her pulse and
respiration are flat, so we need to start—'

'CPR,' he finished, nodding.

Good. They were on the same wavelength.

'I don't speak much Italian. The patient's travelling companion either doesn't speak English or
is too upset to cope in a different language. Can
you ask her if our patient hit her head, is taking
any medication or has any medical conditions?'

'Of course. But first...' He turned to the flight
attendant who'd brought him to the patient. 'We
need your help, please, to fetch supplies. Do you
have an Ambubag and a defibrillator? It should
be kept with the captain.'

'I'll check,' she said, and hurried away.

Then he spoke to their patient's travelling companion in Italian much too rapid for Eleanor to
follow, given the basic Italian she'd started learning
two weeks before. The only word she could catch
was '*dolore*'—what was that? Sorrow?

And then she heard him say '*l'infarto*'—it
sounded close enough to 'infarct', she guessed,

for it to mean 'heart attack'. Usually if a patient was unconscious and there was no pulse, it meant a cardiac arrest—though it could also be a *grand mal* epileptic seizure.

As if Orlando had guessed what she was thinking, he said, 'Our patient's name is Giulietta Russo. She's travelling back to Napoli—Naples—with her daughter Fabiola. Giulietta complained of a pain in her chest and then collapsed. No history of epilepsy, no history of angina, no other medical condition Fabiola can think of, and she didn't hit her head when she collapsed.'

So far, so good. 'Can you ask Fabiola if her mother has a pacemaker?' she asked.

Another burst of rapid Italian. 'No,' he confirmed.

At the same time, Orlando and Eleanor moved the unconscious woman to the aisle and laid her flat. Gently, Eleanor tilted the patient's head and lifted her chin so she could check the airways. 'No sign of blockage. Airway's clear.' But the B and C of 'ABC' were a problem: Giulietta still wasn't breathing and there was still no pulse: no sign of circulation.

'Then we start CPR,' Orlando said. 'You bag and I do the chest compressions, yes? Five compressions to one breath?'

'Thank you,' Eleanor said.

At that moment, the flight attendant arrived with an Ambubag. 'We're still checking for the defibrillator and the drugs kit,' she said.

Eleanor really hoped there was a defibrillator on board. Otherwise their patient had no chance, because even if they landed at the nearest airport it'd take too long to get the help she needed. Without defibrillation, even with CPR, their patient's chances of survival dropped drastically with every minute.

'Thanks,' she said. At least the Ambubag meant that they could give their patient positive pressure ventilation. But when their patient recovered consciousness, she'd need oxygen—more than that available from the aircraft's emergency oxygen masks. 'Is there any supplemental oxygen, please?'

'I'll check,' the flight attendant said, and hurried away again, quickly returning with the defibrillator.

'I'll attach the defibrillator. Do you mind carrying on with the CPR?' she asked Orlando.

They both knew that you couldn't stop the CPR except for the moment when she was ready to administer a shock—if this was a case where she could use a defibrillator. If the monitor showed a different heart rhythm from VF, they were in real trouble.

'No problem,' Orlando said.

Lord, he had a gorgeous smile. The sort that would've made her weak at the knees if she hadn't already been kneeling next to their patient. She glanced up at the flight attendant. 'I need your help to keep doing the breathing while I attach the defibrillator,' she said. 'If Dr de Luca tells you what to do, can you keep going for me, please?'

The other flight attendant nodded, and followed Orlando's instructions while Eleanor attached the defibrillator and checked the monitor reading.

'She's in VF,' she told Orlando, hoping that the abbreviation was the same in his language. Certainly the words would be: ventricular fibrillation, where the heart wasn't contracting properly and was just quivering instead of beating.

She really needed access to Giulietta's neck veins to administer the adrenaline, but in the confines of the aisle space she didn't want to interfere with ventilation. 'I'm going for IV access in the right subclavian vein,' she said to Orlando. 'Administering one milligram of adrenaline. Six-oh-six p.m.'

'Got you.' Although he was a family doctor—a GP—obviously he knew the protocol in this sort of case: one milligram of adrenaline every three minutes. He smiled at her, and kept directing the flight attendant while Eleanor put the paddles of the defibrillator in place.

'Shocking at two hundred joules. Clear,' she said.

As soon as Orlando and the flight attendant had taken their hands off the patient, she administered the shock and continued looking at the readout. 'Still in VF. Charging to two hundred. And clear.'

Another shock. Still no change. 'Still VF. Charging to three-sixty.'

'*Mamma?*' Fabiola asked.

'Um, *bene*. Soon,' Eleanor said, trying to remember the Italian phrases she'd learned and hoping that her voice sounded soothing enough for Fabiola to understand what she meant.

She didn't have time to react to the amusement in Orlando's eyes. 'And clear.'

This time, to her relief, Giulietta responded. 'Sinus rhythm. Can you tell Fabiola that it will be all right? We just need to get her mother to the hospital.'

Orlando nodded, and turned to the flight attendant. 'Can you ask the captain if he can divert the plane to the nearest airport? And talk to the *pronto soccorso* at the hospital—we need the paramedics on standby. *Autoambulanza,*' he added.

Then he talked to Fabiola again in Italian.

'I've explained that her mother needs to go to hospital,' he told Eleanor. 'And we will stay with her until the paramedics can stabilise her.'

It was part and parcel of being a good Samaritan—if there was an emergency and you were present simply as a passer-by and not officially as a doctor, you didn't charge for your service and you stayed with the patient until he or she was stabilised or a doctor with equivalent or higher training took over. Eleanor had heard horror stories of doctors being sued for good Samaritan acts, but she knew if you kept to the protocol and delivered as near to hospital-standard care as you could, you'd be indemnified by either the travel company or your medical union.

The flight attendant who'd been acting as runner came back. 'Captain says he'll land us at Milan. We have clearance, so we should be on the ground in about twenty minutes. The airport's contacting the hospital for us. Oh, and the supplemental oxygen…?'

'Excellent work.' Orlando said with a smile. 'Thank you, *signorina…*?'

The flight attendant blushed. 'Melanie.'

Orlando de Luca was living up to the stereotype, Eleanor thought. Charming every female in the vicinity.

Just like Jeremy.

Well, she wasn't falling for that sort of charm again. Anyway, this relationship was strictly emergency. And strictly medicine. It shouldn't bother her who Orlando de Luca flirted with. It was nothing to do with her.

She busied herself fitting the mask over Giulietta's face.

'Eleanor, your party must be wondering what happened to you.'

Party? Oh. He meant travelling companions. 'It's not a problem, Dr de Luca.'

'Orlando, please.'

Even his name sounded sexy. Her best friend's words echoed in her head: Even if this thing doesn't work out, a week in Italy will do you good. What you need is some Italian glamour...and a fling with a gorgeous man to get that sleazebag Jeremy out of your head.

Tamsin would definitely describe Orlando de Luca as gorgeous. Her exact words would be along the lines of 'sex on legs'. Eleanor couldn't help smiling at the thought.

'My name makes you laugh?'

'No.' Though she certainly wasn't going to explain why she was smiling. What was 'sorry', again? *'Mi dispiace.'*

'You speak some Italian.'

She needed to turn this back to business. Fast. 'A little. But not enough to help Fabiola. Thank you for that. *Grazie.*'

'Prego.' He inclined his head.

At that moment, Giulietta recovered full consciousness and pulled at the mask.

Immediately, Orlando went back into doctor mode, taking her hand and calming her and speaking to her gently in Italian. Eleanor guessed he was telling Giulietta what had happened and where she was going as soon as they reached Milan. She caught the words 'Inglese' and 'dottoressa'—clearly he was explaining who she was, too.

The flight attendants managed to persuade people in the aisle seats to change places with Eleanor and Orlando, so they could continue monitoring Giulietta throughout the descent—both of them were aware that she could easily go back into VF and need shocking again.

But at last they were at the airport. The paramedics boarded the plane with a trolley, and Orlando gave them the full handover details in rapid Italian, pausing every so often to check readings with Eleanor. Fabiola accompanied her mother off the plane, and Eleanor returned to her seat—at the opposite end of the plane to Orlando's.

She wasn't sure whether she was relieved or disappointed when he didn't suggest changing places and sitting with her. Relieved, because then she wouldn't have to make polite conversation and her stomach was already in knots with her impending meeting tomorrow. Yet disappointed, because there was something calming about Orlando—the way he'd assessed the situation, acknowledged that she was the one with emergency experience and hadn't made a fuss about her leading, and had gently turned Fabiola's reaction from panic to understanding. He was the kind of man who made people feel *safe*.

But then again, she knew her judgement in men was lousy. Just because he was a good doctor, it didn't mean he was a good man: Jeremy certainly wasn't. And Orlando was probably married anyway. A man that good-looking couldn't possibly be single. Even if Eleanor was going to act on Tamsin's suggestion of having a holiday fling—which she had no intention of doing—Orlando de Luca wasn't the one for her.

Their paths would probably never cross again, so there was no point in dwelling on it. Besides, she had something else to think about.

Her meeting tomorrow, with the man who might just turn out to be her real father.

And maybe, just maybe, she'd have a family to belong to again. Wouldn't be alone any more.

CHAPTER TWO

THEY were two hours late getting to the airport at Naples. And then there was the wait for the luggage to arrive...except Eleanor couldn't see her suitcase at all.

Maybe she'd just missed it, taken her eye off the conveyor belt during the moment it had passed her, and the suitcase would be there the second time round.

Except it wasn't. Or the third time.

Oh, great. Not only was she late—tired, and in need of a shower and a cup of decent coffee—now her luggage was missing. Thank God she'd put the most important things in her hand luggage. She still had the original photographs back in England, so she could've had replacement copies made, but she'd wanted to hand them over in person.

And although, yes, she could go into the centre

of Naples and replace most of her luggage first thing tomorrow morning, she already had plans. A meeting to which she didn't want to go wearing travel-stained clothes. Even if she rinsed her clothes out in her hotel room tonight, they'd be crumpled and scruffy and...

Oh-h-h.

She could have howled with frustration. The shops were probably closed by now and, even if she got up really early tomorrow morning, she wouldn't have enough time to find the shops, buy new clothes and be on time to meet Bartolomeo.

First impressions were important. Especially in this case. This really, really wasn't fair.

'Problems, Dottoressa Eleanor?'

Orlando's voice was like melted chocolate. Soothing and comforting and sinful, all at the same time.

And she really shouldn't give in to the urge to lean on him. She was perfectly capable of sorting things out on her own. She had a phrasebook in her bag—given a little time and effort, she'd be able to make herself understood. Luggage must go missing all the time. It was probably just mislaid, on the wrong carousel or something.

And when she got to the hotel, she could talk to someone in the reception area and ask where she should go to buy clothes and shoes tomorrow. She could call Bartolomeo and put back their meeting by an hour, if need be.

'I'm just waiting for my luggage,' she said.

'It hasn't arrived yet?'

He was carrying a small, stylish case. And there were only three cases left on the conveyor belt—none of which was hers.

'I was just about to go and ask.'

'Let me,' he said.

Before she could protest, he added, 'You said on the plane that you didn't speak much Italian. So let me help you.'

Italian was his native tongue and he spoke perfect English, too: it made sense to let him interpret for her instead of struggling. '*Grazie.*' Though she still had reservations. 'But won't it make you really late home? Especially as our flight was delayed.'

He shrugged. '*Non importa.* It doesn't matter.'

'It's not fair to your family, to keep them waiting even longer.'

He spread his hands. 'Nobody's waiting for me. I live alone.'

Now, that she hadn't expected. She'd been so sure a man like Orlando de Luca—capable, practical and gorgeous—would be married to a wife who adored him, with several children who adored him even more and a menagerie of dogs and cats he'd rescued over the years.

'I won't be long. What does your bag look like?'

'It's a trolley suitcase—about so big.' She described the size with her hands. 'And it's, um, bright pink.'

'Bright pink,' he echoed. His voice was completely deadpan, but there was a sparkle of amusement in his eyes—as if he thought she'd chosen something completely frivolous and un-doctor-like.

She wished now she'd bought her luggage in a neutral colour. Grey, beige or black. She'd just thought that a bright suitcase would be easier to spot at the airport.

He smiled at her and went over to one of the airport staff. During the conversation, the man nodded, looked over at Eleanor with an expression of respect, said something to Orlando, and then strode away.

'He's going to check for you,' Orlando confirmed when he returned. 'I explained that our flight was late in because of a medical emergency on the plane. You saved the patient's life and we should be looking after you, not losing your baggage.'

She felt colour flood into her face. 'I didn't save Giulietta's life on my own. You did the chest compressions and got a patient history from her daughter. I couldn't have done it without you.'

'Teamwork, then. We worked well together.' His eyes narrowed as he glanced at her. 'You look tired. You've had a long journey, plus the stress of dealing with a cardiac arrest in a cramped space without the kind of equipment you're used to, and now your baggage has disappeared. Come and sit down. I will get you some coffee.'

He was taking over and Eleanor knew she should be standing up for herself, telling him that she appreciated the offer but she really didn't need looking after. Her feelings must have shown on her face because he said gently, 'It may be a while until they locate your luggage. Why stand around waiting and getting stressed, when the coffee-shop is just here, to our right, and you can sit down in comfort and relax?'

And he was right. She *was* tired. Caffeine was just what she needed to get her through the rest of this evening until she got to the hotel.

'Do you take milk, sugar?' he asked when he'd settled her at a table.

'Just milk, please.'

There was something about the English *dottoressa*. Orlando couldn't define it or even begin to put his finger on it, but something about her made him want to get to know her better.

Much better.

He'd liked the way she'd been so cool and calm on the plane, got on with her job without barking orders or being rude to the flight attendants, and had even tried speaking the little Italian she knew to help reassure Giulietta's daughter. There was a warmth to Eleanor Forrest that attracted him.

A warmth that had suddenly shut off when he'd asked her a personal question.

And he wanted to know why.

He ordered coffee and *cantuccini*, then carried a tray over to their table.

'Biscuits?' she asked.

'Because I missed them in England,' he said

simply. 'Your English biscuits fall apart when you dip them in coffee. These don't.' He smiled at her. 'They're nice dipped in *vin santo*, too, but I think for now coffee is what you need.'

'Thanks. Odd how just sitting around can make you feel tired.'

'Don't forget you saved a life in the middle of all that,' he reminded her.

She ignored his comment. 'How much do I owe you for the coffee?'

An independent woman. One who'd insist on paying her way. He liked that, too: she wouldn't take anyone for granted. She was the kind of woman who'd want an equal. 'My suggestion, my bill.'

He caught the expression on her face just before she masked it. Someone had obviously hurt her—hurt her so badly that she wouldn't even accept a cup of coffee from a man she barely knew, and saw strangers as a potential for hurt instead of a potential friend.

Softly, he added, 'That puts you under no obligation to me at all, Eleanor. Whatever you might have heard about Italian men, I can assure you I'm not expecting anything from you. I haven't put anything in your coffee and you're not going to wake up tomorrow morning in a room you can't remember seeing before with no clothes, no money and one hell of a headache.'

'I... I'm sorry. And I didn't mean to insult you or your countrymen,' she said, looking awkward and embarrassed.

'No offence taken. You're quite right to be wary of strangers offering drinks. But I'm a doctor buying a mug of coffee for a fellow professional. And this really is just coffee.'

'And it's appreciated.'

He settled opposite her. 'So, are you on holiday in Naples?'

'Sort of.'

Not a straight yes or no. And she didn't offer any details, he noticed. He had a feeling she'd clam up completely if he pushed her, so he tried for levity instead. 'Your *mamma* told you never to talk to strangers, is that it?'

'No.' Her voice went very quiet. 'Actually, my mother died just before Christmas.'

Six months ago. And the pain was clearly still raw. '*Mi dispiace*, Eleanor,' he said softly. 'I didn't intend to hurt you.'

'You weren't to know. It's not a problem.'

But he noticed she didn't explain any further. And those beautiful brown eyes were filled with sadness. He had a feeling it was more than just grief at losing her mother. Something to do with the man who'd made her wary of strangers, perhaps?

Yet she'd put her feelings aside and gone straight to help a stranger when the flight attendants had asked for a doctor. Eleanor Forrest was an intriguing mixture. And Orlando wanted to know what made her tick.

He switched to a safer topic. 'You're an emergency doctor?'

'Yes.'

OK. He'd try the professional route: say nothing, just smile, and give her space to answer more fully. Just like he did with his shyer patients. If he waited long enough, she'd break the silence.

She did. 'I work in a London hospital.'

Something else they had in common. Good. 'London's a beautiful city. I've just spent a few days there with the doctor I used to share a flat with, Max. It was his son's christening.'

There was the tiniest crinkle round her eyes. 'I don't know if I dare ask. Were you the…?'

'*Padrino?* The godfather, you mean?' So under her reserve there was a sense of fun. He liked that. Enough to want to see more of it. He hummed the opening bars of the theme tune to the film. 'Yes, I was.'

Though seeing the expression on Max's face when he looked at his wife and baby had made Orlando ache. Orlando had stopped believing in love, long ago, when his mother's fifth marriage had crumbled: every time she'd thought she'd found The One, she'd been disillusioned. But Max was so happy with Rachel and little Connor, it had made Orlando think again. Wonder if maybe love really *did* exist.

Except he didn't have a clue where to start looking for it. And he wasn't sure that he wanted to spend his life searching and yearning and getting more and more disappointed, the way his mother did. So he'd decided to stick to the way he'd lived for the last five years—smile, keep his relationships light, just for fun, and put his energy into his work.

'You work in London, too?' she asked.

'Not any more. I did, for a couple of years, on a children's ward.' He spread his hands. 'But then I discovered I wanted to see my patients grow up—not forget about them once they'd left the hospital. I wanted to treat them, just as I'd treated their parents and their grandparents and would treat their children. I wanted to see them with their families.'

Strange, really, when he didn't have a family of his own. Just his mother, a few ex-stepfathers and ex-stepsiblings he hadn't kept in touch with. The only way he'd get an extended family now was to get married: and that was a risk he wasn't prepared to take.

Keep it light, he reminded himself. 'And I missed the lemon groves. I missed the sea.'

'And the sunshine,' she said with a wry smile.

'I don't mind London rain. But I admit, although I like visiting London, it's good to be back under the Italian sun. And I love being a family doctor.'

She smiled, and he caught his breath. Her serious manner masked her beauty—when she smiled, Eleanor Forrest was absolutely stunning. Perfect teeth and a wide smile and those amazing deep brown eyes.

It made him want to touch her. Trace the

outline of her face with the tips of his fingers. Rub his thumb against her lower lip. And then dip his head to hers, claiming her mouth.

Then he became aware she was speaking. Oh, lord. He really hoped he hadn't ignored a question or something. She must think he was a real idiot.

'My best friend at medical school, Tamsin, did the same thing,' Eleanor said. 'She started in paediatrics and became a GP because she wanted to care for the whole family.'

'There's a lot to be said for it.' But they were talking about him. He wanted to know about *her*. 'You prefer the buzz of emergency medicine?'

'I like knowing I've made a difference,' she said simply.

She'd make a difference all right, he thought. Whatever branch of medicine she worked in. But before he could say anything, the man he'd spoken to about Eleanor's luggage came over, carrying one bright pink case.

'I am sorry for the wait, Dottoressa Forrest,' he said politely.

'No problem. *Grazie,*' she said, taking the case and checking the label. 'Yes, this is mine.'

He left after some pleasantries, and Eleanor stood up. 'Thank you for the coffee, Dottore de Luca.'

'You haven't finished it yet.'

She made a face. 'It's getting late. I really ought to check into my hotel.'

He didn't want her to walk out of his life. Not yet. And there was one way he could keep her talking to him for a little longer. 'You could be waiting a while for a taxi, and although public transport is good in Naples, you have baggage with you. I'll give you a lift.'

She shook her head. 'Thank you, but you've already been kind enough. I'd rather not impose.'

He wasn't sure what was going on here—he'd never experienced this weird, unexplainable feeling before—but what he knew for definite was that if he let her walk out of his life now, he'd regret it. Somehow he needed to persuade her to trust him. And to spend time with him so they could get to know each other.

Max had said he'd known the instant he'd met Rachel that she was the one he wanted to spend the rest of his life with. Orlando had scoffed, saying it was just lust and luckily he'd found friendship as well. But now he wasn't so sure.

Was it possible to fall in love with someone at first sight? Did 'The One' exist? Was this odd feeling love? And was Eleanor Forrest the one he'd been waiting for?

He needed to know.

Needed to keep her with him.

'Eleanor, I know I'm a stranger, but you're a fellow doctor and you've helped save the life of one of my countrymen. Don't they say in England, one good turn deserves another?'

Eleanor couldn't help smiling at the old-fashioned phrase. 'You've already bought me coffee and sorted out my luggage for me. I think we're quits.'

'Let me put this another way. You could take a taxi, but why spend money you could spend on…' he waved an impatient hand '…oh, good coffee or ice cream or something frivolous to make your time here in Italy fun, when I can give you a lift?'

Lord, it was tempting. But she knew it would be a bad idea. Orlando de Luca might be the most attractive man she'd met in a long while—probably ever, if she thought about it—but that didn't mean she should act on the attraction. She'd already proved her judgement in men was lousy. Spectacularly lousy. OK, so Jeremy had caught her at an acutely vulnerable moment, but she'd still swallowed every single lie. Not just hook, line and sinker—more like the whole fishing rod. 'We might not be going the same way.'

'Then again, we might.'

The man should've been a lawyer. He had an answer for everything.

'So where are you going?' he asked.

A direct question. One she was reluctant to answer.

He lifted an eyebrow. 'Is it all strangers, all men, or just me?'

She frowned. 'How do you mean?'

'I make you nervous, Eleanor.'

'No.' Actually, that wasn't quite true. He *did* make her nervous. Because she was aware of the chemistry between them. And she remembered what had happened last time she'd acted on chemistry. Cue one broken heart. And she was still picking up the pieces.

'There's another saying in your country, is there not?' he asked softly. 'Trust me, I'm a doctor.'

Ha. Jeremy had proved that one to be false in

the extreme. He was a doctor—and most definitely not to be trusted.

She faced Orlando, ready to be firm and say thank you but, no—she was getting a taxi. And then she saw the challenge in his eyes. As if he dared her to take the risk. Let him drive her to the hotel.

They'd worked well together on the plane. She'd trusted him then. Could she trust him now?

'I won't expect you to invite me in for a nightcap, if that's what you're worrying about.'

She felt the colour shoot into her face. 'Actually, that didn't occur to me.' Though Orlando had already told her he was single. And he was the most gorgeous man she'd seen in years, with those unruly dark curls, dark expressive eyes and a mouth that promised all kinds of pleasure. And she couldn't get Tamsin's suggestion out of her head: that a holiday fling with a gorgeous man would do her good...

He folded his arms. 'So are you going to stand in a long, long queue, Dottoressa Eleanor, or are you going to let me drop you off on my way home?'

She gave in to temptation. 'If you're sure it's no trouble, then thank you. A lift would be nice.'

His smile was breathtaking. And it made every single one of her nerve-endings feel as if it were purring.

'Then let's go through Customs, *tesoro*,' he said softly.

The queues at the customs area and passport control had died down, and they moved through the airport surprisingly quickly. She followed Orlando into the car park—just as she could've guessed, he drove a low-slung, shiny black car. A convertible, to be exact. Men and their toys. And didn't they say that all Italian men wanted to be racing-car drivers?

As if her thoughts were written all over her face, he laughed and stowed her case in the boot next to his. 'I have only myself to please, Eleanor. And I love driving along the coast road with the hood down and the wind in my hair and the scent of the sea and lemon groves every-where. If you have time in your schedule here, maybe you'd like to come with me some time.'

He made it sound so inviting.

And it made her knees go weak to imagine it: Orlando, wearing a black T-shirt and black jeans, a pair of dark glasses covering his eyes, at the wheel of the open-topped car.

'So, your hotel?'

She told him the name, and before she could tell him the address he told her exactly where it was. Clearly he knew his home city well. 'And just to stop you feeling guilty about taking me out of my way, it's on my side of the city. On my way home, to be precise. It's within walking distance of my apartment, in the Old Quarter.' He opened the passenger door for her, an old-fashioned gesture of courtesy she found charming.

Though some nervousness must have shown on her face because he added, 'I assure you, Eleanor, you will be perfectly safe. I am a good driver.'

He proved it. Though he was also a very fast driver, and her knuckles were white by the time he pulled up outside her hotel.

'We are both in one piece,' he said with a grin. 'Relax.'

She wasn't sure if it was the way he'd driven—exactly the same as all the other people on the road, taking advantage of every little gap in the traffic—or being so close to him in such a small space, but relaxing was the last thing she felt like doing right now.

'Enjoy your stay in Italy, Eleanor.' When he'd

taken her case from the back of his car and carried it up the steps to the entrance of the hotel, he took a card from his wallet, and scribbled a number on the back of it. 'If you have some spare time while you are in Naples, maybe we could have dinner. My surgery number is on the front. The one I've written on the back is my mobile. Call me.'

It wasn't a question.

'Call me,' he said again, his voice soft, and raised her hand to his mouth.

The brush of his lips against her skin was momentary. It was a mere courtesy, she knew, the Italian way of doing things. It didn't mean anything. But there was heat in his eyes. Heat matched by the flicker of desire rising up her spine.

Calling him would be way too dangerous for her peace of mind. But she wasn't going to argue over it now. Instead, she smiled politely. 'Thank you for the lift, Dottore de Luca.'

'Orlando,' he corrected. *'Prego.'* He smiled, sketched a bow, ran lightly down the steps to his car and drove off.

CHAPTER THREE

ONCE Eleanor had signed the register and been shown to her room, she unpacked swiftly and took a shower. She was too tired and it was too late to eat a proper meal, so she ordered a milky hot chocolate from room service. She started to text her mum to say she'd arrived safely, then realised what she was doing halfway through, blinked away the tears, reminded herself to stop being over-emotional and texted Tamsin instead.

When she'd finished her hot chocolate, she slid into bed and curled into a ball. The sheets were cool and smooth and the bed was comfortable, but despite the milky drink she couldn't sleep.

Because she couldn't get a certain face out of her mind. Orlando de Luca. Every time she closed her eyes she saw his face. His smile. That hot look in his eyes.

Which was crazy.

Right now she wasn't in the market for a relationship. She knew she needed to get over Jeremy's betrayal and move on with her life, but was having a holiday fling with a gorgeous man really the right way to do that? And anyway there must be some reason why Orlando was single.

She didn't think it was a personality flaw—the way he'd worked with her was nothing like the way Jeremy worked, being so charming that you didn't realise until it was too late that he'd taken the credit for everything. Orlando was genuine. A nice guy, as well as one of the most attractive he'd ever met.

So why? He'd said he'd worked as a paediatrician then turned to family medicine. So was he still building his career and putting his love life on hold until he was where he wanted to be? Was he the sort who was dedicated to his career and didn't want the commitment to a relationship? In that case he would be the perfect fling—and maybe she should call him…

But not until after her meeting tomorrow. Her stomach tightened with nerves. What would Bartolomeo Conti be like? He'd sounded nice, on the phone. The photograph he'd emailed to her was that of a man in his mid-fifties with a charming smile. But she knew firsthand that charm often covered something far less pleasant. And her mother hadn't stayed with Bartolomeo. So was the man who might be her father a snake beneath the smile? Or was she judging him unfairly?

Finally, Eleanor fell asleep; the next morning, the alarm woke her, and by the time she'd showered her stomach was in knots. She couldn't face even the usual light Italian breakfast of a crumbly pastry, just a frothy cappuccino—and she checked her watch what turned out to be every thirty seconds to make sure she wasn't going to be late.

After one last glance in the mirror in her room to check she looked respectable, she headed for the hotel lounge. The second she walked in, a tall man stood up and waved to her. She recognised him instantly from the photo he'd emailed her— just as he'd clearly recognised her.

A moment of panic. What did she call him? 'Signor Conti?'

'Bartolomeo,' he corrected. 'And I hope you will let me call you Eleanor.' He enveloped her in a hug. 'Thank you so much for coming to see me—and all this way, from London.'

'*Prego.*'

He looked delighted that she'd made the effort to speak his language. 'We are both early.' His smile turned slightly wry. 'I slept badly.'

'Me, too,' she admitted.

He put his hands on her shoulders and looked closely at her. 'I thought it from your photo, and now I know for sure. You look so much like my Costanza. Constance Firth,' he corrected, 'the woman I fell in love with, thirty years ago.' He added softly, 'But your colouring is all mine.'

Constance Forrest had been fair-haired and Tim Forrest had had sandy hair; both had been blue-eyed. What were the chances of them producing a brown-eyed, dark-haired child—one with olive skin that didn't burn, rather than an English rose? Whereas Bartolomeo Conti, the man whose initial had been at the bottom of the love letter she'd found among her mother's things, had hair, skin and eyes the same colour as her own. Coincidence? Or was he her biological father?

'Have you had breakfast, Eleanor?' he asked.

She shook her head. 'I was too nervous to eat.'

'Me, too. Let's go and have a late breakfast and watch the world go by.'

He took her to a little caffè-bar and ordered them both coffee and *sfogliatelle*. 'You will like these, Eleanor—they are a Neapolitan speciality. Sweet pastry shaped like a shell and filled with sweetened ricotta cheese and candied orange rind.' His smile was full of memories. 'I bought these for your *mamma,* the first time we went to a *caffè* together.'

She had so many questions. But they had time.

'I thought you might like to see these,' Eleanor said when they'd sat down, handing him an envelope.

Bartolomeo leafed through them. 'Yes, this is how I remember my Costanza,' he said softly. 'And she grew into a very, very beautiful woman. This one of her in the garden…' There was a catch in his voice. 'And this is you as a *bambina*?' He smiled. 'You look so much like my sisters Luisella and Federica when they were *bambini*. Those dimples… May I borrow these to make copies?'

'Keep them. I did this set for you,' Eleanor explained.

He reached over the table and hugged her. 'I never thought I would be blessed with children. And now…' He shook his head in wonder. 'And now it seems I have a daughter. A daughter I would very much like to get to know. If your *papà* does not mind?'

She appreciated the fact he'd asked. Even though strictly speaking it didn't matter any more. 'Dad had a stroke the year after I graduated as a doctor.' Though at least Tim Forrest had been there for her graduation. He'd shared that particular triumph with her. 'There's only me now.'

'You are alone in the world?' Bartolomeo looked shocked. 'What of Costanza's *famiglia*? Her mother, her father?'

'I never knew them.'

He frowned. 'Are you telling me they disowned Costanza because she had you when she was not married?'

Eleanor shook her head. 'I don't really know anything about them. The only grandparents I remember were dad's parents, but he was twenty years older than Mum and they died when I was in my early teens.' She'd often wondered about her grandparents but hadn't wanted to hurt her mother by asking. And, thirty years ago, being pregnant and unmarried had still had a bit of a stigma. So maybe Bartolomeo's theory was right. 'You really had no idea I existed?'

'None,' he said firmly. 'Had I known my Costanza was carrying my baby, I would have flown straight to England and married her.'

'So what happened?' She needed to know. Why had her mother gone back to England alone?

Bartolomeo sighed. 'I don't come out of it very well, but I want to be honest with you from the start. I fell in love with your mother, but I wasn't really free to do so.' He looked awkward. 'I wasn't formally betrothed to Mariella, the daughter of my father's business partner, but we'd grown up together and our families both expected us to get married. Except then I met Costanza. She was on holiday. It was springtime. I drove past her and caught her in a shower from a puddle. I stopped and took her for a coffee to apologise and that was it. Love at first sight.'

Something she didn't believe in—in her view, you had to get to know someone properly first—so why couldn't she get Orlando de Luca out of her head?

Memories softened Bartolomeo's face. 'Your mother was so warm, so vibrant—nothing like the cool English rose I thought she would be when I first heard her accent. She made me laugh, and I fell in love with her smile. We were inseparable in the days after that. Everything happened very fast, and I knew I wanted to marry her. I told my parents that I could not marry Mariella, that I wanted my bright English girl. And it was made very clear to me that I would have to choose between my family and Costanza.'

'So you chose your family.' Eleanor could understand that. She would've hated being cut off from her parents.

'Not at all. I told them if they were going to insist I had to choose, then I would choose my Costanza.' Bartolomeo's face tightened. 'But she had already made the decision for me. I went to her hotel and she was gone. She'd left me a letter, saying she would not come between me and my family. She was going back to England and she wasn't going to see me again. And I was to marry Mariella, as everyone expected, and be happy.'

Which had given him a neat get-out. And even

though Bartolomeo had warned her he didn't come out of it well, disappointment seeped through her.

'Didn't you even *try* to get in touch with her?'

'Of course I did. But I didn't have a telephone number for her, only an address.' He frowned. 'I wrote to her but my letters were returned unopened.'

'And that was it? You just gave up?'

He smiled wryly. 'You have to remember, I wasn't that old. I was twenty-two. So I did the impulsive thing and flew over to England. I thought that I could make her change her mind if I saw her—but when I arrived your grandparents told me she had moved out and they wouldn't give me a forwarding address. I didn't know who her friends were, where she worked, where even to start finding her. And then I thought, clearly, she meant it. She really didn't want to see me again or she would have left me clues.' He looked sad. 'And now I know I was right. She decided to keep it a clean break. Otherwise she would have told me about you. My Costanza was never a liar.'

'But she never told *me* about *you*. I grew up thinking Dad was…' She shrugged. 'Well, my dad. I only started wondering when I bought my house and the bank queried the fact my birth certificate had my surname as Firth. Mum said it was just an admin thing. Then, when I was clearing out her things afterwards, I found the papers: they changed my name from Firth to Forrest by deed poll after they married.'

'So her husband brought you up as his own.' Bartolomeo looked anxious. 'She was happy with him? He treated her well? Treated you both well?'

There was a lump in Eleanor's throat as she remembered. 'They loved each other very, very much. And, yes, they were happy. *We* were happy. We were a family.' The perfect family. And how she missed them.

'I am glad.' Her surprise must have shown on her face because he said, 'I would not want my Costanza to be sad. And I would want your childhood to be full of smiles.'

'It was. Tim obviously wasn't my biological father, but he was my dad. He read me bedtime stories, taught me to ride a bike and drive a car, grilled my boyfriends and grounded me when I was late home, helped me with my homework and opened the champagne when I got my exam results. He was always there any time I needed to talk—always there with a hug and a smile and sheer common sense when I was full of teenage angst. Mum was, too.' She swallowed back the tears, the aching loss. The knowledge that Tim would've seen through Jeremy and gently made her see the truth. 'And you? You were happy with Mariella?'

'We married, but it was a mistake.' He sighed. 'I loved her, but not in the way I loved Costanza—there wasn't the same spark, the same passion I found with Costanza. We were more…friends. I tried to be a good husband, worked hard to provide for her and build up my family's business. Too hard, maybe, because she thought I neglected her.' He shrugged. 'She found love in someone else's arms.'

'I'm sorry.'

He sipped his coffee. 'No matter. But I've had my work, and my sisters are close to me. And I have two nieces to spoil.' He smiled. 'And you? You have a husband, a *fidanzato*?'

She'd had a fiancé. Five months ago. 'No. I'm single.'

'A beautiful *ragazza* like you? Why?'

'There was someone,' she admitted.

'What happened?'

'He was wrong for me.' She wasn't prepared to tell Bartolomeo just how close she'd been to making the biggest mistake of her life. If she hadn't met Penelope and found out the truth… She pushed the thought away. 'So what made you send that message to the radio station?'

'To find my lost love? I've reached that age when you look back at your life and you wonder what you would have done differently.' He spread his hands. 'I am just lucky you heard the *Lost Loves* programme.'

'And put the pieces together.' She nodded. 'That song always made Mum cry. And the dates fitted—the summer before I was born. I never even knew she'd been to Italy.'

'I regret that I never knew you as a baby.' His voice softened. 'I can't change the past. But we can change the future. And I would very much like you to be part of my future, Eleanor. Part of my family.'

Longing tugged at her. To be part of a family again…how could she say no?

* * *

Before Eleanor knew it, it was lunchtime. She and Bartolomeo ate a leisurely *panini* and fruit and ordered more coffee, and spent their time talking and catching up.

Finally she glanced at her watch. 'I'm sorry—have I made you late for an appointment?'

Bartolomeo smiled. 'I kept my diary free today.' But he looked pale, tired. 'Are you all right?' she asked.

'Just getting old—at the stage in my life where I need a *sonnelino*, a nap.'

But Bartolomeo could only be in his early fifties. If he'd been twenty-two when her mother had fallen pregnant, that would make him fifty-three now. He was too young to feel this tired, this early in the day.

'Come to dinner tonight,' he said. He took a business card from a small leather case, and wrote swiftly on the back. 'This is my address. My sisters and their husbands usually come over for supper on a Tuesday evening. Come and meet them.'

Eleanor wasn't sure. 'It's the evening you spend with your family.'

'You are my daughter. So they are your family,

too.' He smiled and squeezed her hand. 'It's nothing formal—a simple supper. Please come.'

'I...'

'Please?'

How could she resist that beseeching look? 'All right.'

He beamed at her. 'Then I will see you at seven, yes?'

Once his taxi had driven off, Eleanor headed into the centre of Naples. For a mad moment she thought about calling Orlando—but he was probably in surgery right now. And anyway, she wasn't there to have a holiday fling: she was there to find out the truth about her father. She really didn't need the extra complication.

She wasn't sure whether the etiquette of dinner parties was the same in Italy as it was in England, but she bought wine and chocolates to take with her anyway. She'd just finished changing when the phone in her room rang.

'Dottoressa Forrest? I have a call for you,' the receptionist said.

Odd. If it was Tamsin, the call would've come through on her mobile phone. Who would call her at the hotel? Bartolomeo, to cancel this evening? 'Thank you. I'll take it,' she said quietly.

'Hello, Eleanor?'

She recognised the voice immediately, and a shiver of pure pleasure ran down her spine. 'Orlando?'

'I was just passing your hotel on my way home. Do you have time to have a drink with me in the bar?'

She glanced at her watch. Fifteen minutes until she needed to catch the metro. Fifteen minutes when she could sit on her own and worry about whether Bartolomeo's family would accept her, or… 'I have to leave in about fifteen minutes,' she said.

'Then you do have time. *Bene.* What would you like to drink?'

She knew that alcohol wasn't the right way to soothe her nerves: she didn't want to turn up at dinner reeking of wine the first time she met the Conti family. 'Mineral water would be lovely. Sparkling, please. I'll be right down.'

She replaced the receiver, picked up the things she wanted to take with her to Bartolomeo's, and went to join Orlando in the bar. He was sitting at a table on his own, skimming through a newspaper and seemingly oblivious to the admiring glances of the women sitting in the bar. Including her own. In a well-cut dark suit with a sober tie and a white shirt, he looked absolutely edible. As she reached the table, he put down the newspaper and stood up. 'Thank you for joining me, Eleanor.'

Old-fashioned etiquette. Funny how it made her knees weak.

'I assumed you'd like ice and lemon,' he said, indicating the glass at the place opposite him.

'*Grazie,*' she said, sitting down.

'*Prego.*' He smiled at her, sat down and poured water from the bottle into her glass. 'I rang the hospital in Milan today. I thought you'd like to know that Giulietta Russo is doing just fine and they expect her to make a full recovery from her heart attack.'

She smiled back. 'That's great news. Thanks for telling me.'

'Though I admit, it wasn't the only reason I called by.' He took a sip of his own drink—also mineral water, she noticed. 'I wondered if you might be free the day after tomorrow—if you'd like to come to Pompeii with me.'

He was asking her on a date?

Her first thought was, *Yes, please.* Her second was more sensible: despite Tamsin's suggestion, she really wasn't here in Naples to have a fling. And the fact that she hadn't been able to stop thinking about Orlando meant she really ought to steer clear: things could get way too complicated, and right now there were enough complications in her life.

She took a sip of iced water to give her a breathing space. The answer was no—but nicely. Because in other circumstances it would definitely have been yes.

'It's very kind of you to ask,' she said, 'but I'm not in the market for a date.'

He looked pointedly at her left hand. 'Not married. So you're involved with someone at home—someone who couldn't join you here in Italy?'

'No. I'm single,' she admitted.

'As am I. So what's the harm? You're here on holiday, yes?'

'Not exactly,' she hedged.

'Business, then?'

She shook her head. 'It's personal. But I can't

really talk about it right now. I need to get some things straight in my head.'

'It sounds,' Orlando said thoughtfully, 'as if you could use a friend. A sounding-board, you could say. Someone who's not involved.'

Lord, he was acute. That was exactly what she needed. Someone who was objective, who could see things more clearly than she could right now.

'You barely know me, I admit—but I think we could be friends. And, as a *medico di famiglia*, I'm a good listener.' He spread his hands. 'Come to Pompeii with me. We can potter around among the ruins and eat *gelati*...and you can talk to me, knowing that whatever you tell me won't go any further.'

Tempting. So tempting

But Eleanor wasn't sure she could handle the beginning of a relationship as well as everything else—even if it was just temporary, a holiday fling.

'As friends,' he added, almost as if he'd guessed why she was stalling. 'No pressure.'

She nodded. 'Then thank you. I'd like that.'

'Good.' His eyes glittered. 'I'll pick you up here the day after tomorrow, at half past ten. Do you have good walking shoes?'

'Yes.'

'Wear them.' Then, to take the edge off the command, he gave her one of those slow, sensual, knee-buckling smiles—a smile that made her very glad she was sitting down. 'Of course, you could wear high heels if you prefer. But you'd end up with blisters.'

Which he, as a doctor, would insist on treating. The idea of his fingers stroking her skin—even if it was only to put a protective plaster around a blister—made desire flicker through her.

He glanced at his watch. 'My fifteen minutes is up. Unless you can be late?'

She shook her head. 'Not this time. It's…complicated.'

'You don't have to explain, *bella mia*.' He reached across the table, took her hand, raised it to his lips and kissed it—just the way he had the previous day, when he'd dropped her off at the hotel.

Every nerve-ending seemed to heat, and, shockingly, she found herself wondering what it would be like to feel his mouth against her own instead of her hand.

Oh, lord.

'Thank you for the drink,' she said politely. 'And I'm sorry I didn't, um, have a chance to finish it.'

'*Non importa.* You warned me we only had fifteen minutes.' He smiled at her. 'Have a pleasant evening. And I will see you on Thursday morning, yes?'

'Thursday.' And she really hoped her voice didn't sound as croaky to him as it did to her.

CHAPTER FOUR

THE evening went better than Eleanor had expected: Bartolomeo's sisters were a little wary of her to start with, but gradually started to thaw. She spent Wednesday morning exploring the city and the afternoon with Bartolomeo.

And then it was Thursday morning.

Her date-that-wasn't-a-date with Orlando.

She knew the second that he walked into the hotel foyer—even though she was reading a guidebook to Pompeii rather than watching the door—because the air in the room changed. Became electric.

And she noticed that just about every woman in the room was watching him as he walked towards her. His movements were fluid, graceful—almost like a dancer's. Beautiful. Yet he didn't seem aware of the turned heads. He just came to a stop in front of her and smiled.

'*Buon giorno*, Eleanor. You are ready?'

'Sure.' She closed the guidebook and stuffed it into her handbag.

'Then let's go.' He held his hand out to pull her to her feet. 'So, today—on your holiday that isn't exactly a holiday—you are officially on holiday, yes?'

The convoluted phrasing made her laugh—and made her realise how ridiculous she was being. There was no need to be cagey about why she was there. And, given what Orlando did for a living...she could do with a second medical opinion to confirm her suspicions. 'Yes.'

'*Bene.*' He ushered her down the steps to where he'd parked the car, and opened the door for her. She hid a smile. All the women were staring at them and envying her for being with someone so gorgeous. And all the men were staring at them and envying her for climbing into a car that gorgeous. Well, they were probably envying Orlando, actually, for being behind the wheel.

'What?' Orlando asked as he closed the driver's door.

'Nothing.'

He tipped his head on one side. 'Nothing?'

'Your car's attracting attention, that's all.'

He shrugged. 'There are plenty of cars like this in Italy.'

A low-slung, sleek black convertible. 'Flashy.'

He slanted her a grin. 'I prefer to use the word "fun".'

He would. 'Why are we driving there? The tourist guide said the best way to get to Pompeii is by train.' Driving in Naples would be a nightmare. Full of traffic jams—worse even than London, she thought.

'Ah, so you were reading while you were waiting for me?' He laughed. 'It's true—but I wanted to take you along the coast afterwards. So this saves time coming back to Naples. This is your first time in Naples, I take it?'

'My first time in Italy, full stop,' she said.

He smiled. 'You chose the best place. Rome is flashy. Venice is…' he made a noise of contempt '…flooded.'

She laughed. 'Isn't that the point?'

'Maybe, but they also have *alta acqua*. Which is very far from pleasant, believe me.' He shuddered. 'Naples—now, we have Vesuvius. And the bay. We have the most beautiful churches in Italy. Oh, and the best pizza. Best *gelati*, too.'

She grinned. 'I'll take it as read that you love your home city, then.'

'That's why I came back,' he said simply. 'Don't get me wrong—I was happy in London. But this is home.'

'It's sort of my home too, in a way.'

'How so?'

He sounded interested, yet not pushy, and she found herself telling him. 'I never knew but my mother came here the year before I was born. She fell in love with someone. It didn't work out. But then I heard my mother's name on this radio programme—one of these ones where people search for their lost loves—and it was the man she'd fallen in love with. So I got in touch.'

'And you're here to meet him?'

'Yes.' She paused. 'That's why I said I wasn't really here on holiday. Because it turns out that he's my biological father.'

'And you had no idea?'

'Not until after my mother died, no. I mean, you hear of these "secret babies"—but you don't expect to find out that you're one of them.'

'It must have been a shock for you,' he said, sounding sympathetic. 'You were meeting him for the first time the other night?'

'Second,' she said. 'This time, I met his family.'

'Ouch. Difficult for you,' he said.

'More difficult for them—this English girl appearing out of nowhere after thirty years and claiming to be related.'

'We have warm hearts and big families over here. Give it time. They'll get used to the idea.' He reached over with his right hand and squeezed her hand. 'You're very brave to come all this way on your own. You told me about your mother, but you have no brothers, no sisters?'

'Just me. And my dad—the man who brought me up, the man I've always thought of as my dad—died the year after I graduated.'

Orlando left his hand curled round hers. 'So this man—your biological father—is now your only family.'

'Something like that.'

'So what about your friend, the one who's a GP? Wouldn't she come with you?'

'She would have done—but she's six months pregnant.'

The penny clearly dropped. 'So no travelling.'

She shrugged. 'There's just me.'

'Just you,' he said softly.

She swallowed hard. 'Except... Can I ask your advice?'

'Of course.'

'Bartolomeo said he'd just reached that age when he's curious about what might have been—that's why he tried to find Mum. But I think there's more to it than that. He isn't *that* old—he's in his early fifties, the prime of his life. And yet he's tiring easily, he's pale and I've noticed that he gets a little out of breath when he walks. That's not normal. So I'm thinking either a heart condition or maybe AML.' Without examining him herself, she couldn't give a proper diagnosis. But the symptoms she'd noticed were definitely worrying. 'And I was wondering...maybe he wanted to find Mum to make his peace with her. Before...' Her throat closed up and she couldn't say the words.

Orlando clearly knew what she meant, because the pressure of his hand tightened briefly around hers. 'It might be a post-viral illness—he might be recovering, not becoming sicker,' he said.

'But I think you need to talk to him about it. Be open about it. Get him to put your mind at rest.'

'Or let me prepare for the worst.'

'You,' Orlando told her, 'are looking on the dark side. It might not be what you think. You know as well as I do that the symptoms you listed apply to other illnesses that can be cured, or at least controlled. The breathlessness could be asthma—which can start at any age, so it could be recent and he's not used to taking his inhalers yet.'

'Maybe.'

'Talk to him,' Orlando advised. 'And although my medical textbooks are in Italian so they won't be much use to you, if you need them for research I can translate for you.'

'That's a very generous offer.' She was glad that her sunglasses hid her need to blink back tears.

'We're friends. Well, maybe we're more acquaintances, at the moment,' he told her, 'but we're going to be friends. And friends look out for each other, yes?'

'Thank you. *Grazie.*'

He smiled. 'My pleasure, *tesoro*. And now I want you to stop worrying. Until you've talked to him and found more information, there's nothing you can do. So relax. Enjoy the sunshine. Things have a way of working out.'

He squeezed her hand once more, then placed his hand back on the steering-wheel. This time he drove a little more sedately than he had from the airport. And then she noticed the music playing softly in the background. A string quartet: something she didn't recognise, but it was soothing—and very pretty. 'What's the music?' she asked

'Vivaldi.'

'It's lovely.'

'Well, of course. It's Italian.' He gave her a wicked look. 'We do have more than just "O Sole Mio", you know.'

'You listen to mainly classical music?'

'Depends on my mood. I'll sing along with Lucio Battisti or Andrea Bocelli—or sometimes I just like the regularity of Vivaldi or Corelli in the background. Had I been a surgeon, I think I would choose this for the operating theatre.' He paused. 'And you?'

She shrugged. 'Whatever's on the radio. Something I can hum along to.'

'If you want to change the music, help yourself.'

Jeremy had teased her about singing out of key: no way was she going to sing along in the car beside a man she barely knew. A man she was finding more and more attractive, the more time she spent with him. Today Orlando was wearing casual clothes—pale linen trousers and a white T-shirt—and yet he looked utterly gorgeous. Even more so than he had in a formal suit—because casual meant *touchable*.

And he'd just been holding her hand.

She gripped the edges of her sunhat to keep herself from temptation.

'I'm glad you don't have long hair,' Orlando said.

Not what the rest of the world had said when she'd gone from hair that was almost waist-length to an urchin cut. 'Oh?'

'Because it's beautiful outside,' he said. 'Beautiful enough to have the top down—but if your hair were long and loose, that wouldn't be much fun for you.'

'Is that a hint?'

'Would you mind? I know it's hot, but we're not that far from Pompeii so you shouldn't get a headache from the sun. Though I would advise you to remove your hat.'

She did as he suggested. *'Prego.'*

He pressed a button: moments later, the hood was down and folded away. Automatic. Impressive.

'Now you're showing off,' she said.

He laughed. 'It's called "having fun".'

When they reached Pompeii, Orlando put the hood back up, and took two bottles of water from the glove compartment.

'You need to keep properly hydrated in this climate,' he said.

'Thanks. I didn't think about that.'

He shrugged. 'At least you remembered a hat and sunglasses. That's more than many people would.'

'And as you drove us here,' she told him when they joined the queue for tickets, 'I'm paying the entrance fee.'

'No. This was my idea. And in my world women don't pay on a date.'

'This isn't a date,' she reminded him. 'We're here as friends. I pay for the tickets, or no deal.'

He laughed. 'You're independent and impossible. And I want the pleasure of showing you Pompeii, so what choice do I have?' He held his hand out for her to shake. 'OK, it's a deal. Provided you let me buy you a *gelati.*'

She shook his hand, and her palm tingled at the contact. 'Deal,' she said, hearing the huskiness in her own voice and hoping that Orlando hadn't noticed.

When she'd paid for their tickets, they wandered through into the old town. There were beautiful frescoes and mosaic floors everywhere. 'It's gorgeous. You wouldn't think this place was over two thousand years old,' she said, full of wonder.

'Nearer three,' Orlando said, 'as it was first occupied in the eighth century BC. Some of the ruined buildings were actually ruins before the eruption.'

'Incredible.' Though there was something that made her uncomfortable. 'Those bodies on the floor…where did they come from?'

'They're plaster casts,' he told her. 'The ash from the volcano fell and buried the people and animals, then hardened round them. The bodies decomposed and left a space behind in the ash. In the nineteenth century, the archaeologist Giuseppi Fiorelli had the idea of pumping plaster in to the cavities so we could see what was under the ash.'

'That's a bit ghoulish,' Eleanor said. 'I mean, these were people—we're witnessing how they suffered, their last agonies. It's a bit...well, not very nice, don't you think?'

He gave her a perceptive look. 'Is that why you became an emergency doctor? To stop people hurting?'

She nodded. 'Neither of my parents were medics. Dad was a history teacher and Mum taught music.'

'Your father would have enjoyed it here, then.'

'Loved it,' she confirmed. 'He used to research local history for fun and would spend hours in the archives. He did some research in the National Archives at Kew while I was training in London. I remember he met me from lectures and we had dinner together.' The memories were good, but they still made tears clog her throat—because they made her realise how much she missed her parents.

'You were close to your parents?' Orlando asked.

She nodded. 'Very. I miss them.' She shook herself. 'How about you? Are your parents medics?'

He shrugged. 'My mother is in property.'

He didn't say anything about his father, she

noticed, and there were lines of tension around his mouth. Clearly she'd just prodded a very sore point. Maybe, she thought, his father had died when Orlando had been young.

On impulse, she took his hand and squeezed it. '*Mi dispiace*, Orlando. I was being nosy. I'm sorry if I've said something that brought back sad memories.'

'*Non importa.* It doesn't matter.'

But he laced his fingers through hers and didn't let her hand go. Oddly, it felt *right*. If someone had said to her a week ago that she'd been strolling hand in hand with a gorgeous Italian between Vesuvius and the sea, she would've laughed—but it was happening.

She'd learned that making plans—as she had with Jeremy—didn't work for her. So from now she was going to do the opposite: take things as they came. Enjoy life as she experienced it.

And sauntering through Pompeii with Orlando was fantastic. Especially as he seemed to know everything about the site—pointed out little things that she wouldn't have noticed and which she couldn't remember seeing in the guide book she'd started reading the previous evening.

The streets were rough; she stumbled slightly on a paving slab, and Orlando steadied her against him. 'OK?' he asked.

Very OK. Holding hands with Orlando—even though she knew that it didn't mean anything—sent a warm glow through her. Something about his strength, his steadiness. Orlando de Luca was the kind of man who'd never let you down. 'I'm fine.'

'Good.' He didn't let go of her hand. 'The roads used to flood here, so they made special pedestrian crossings of raised stones to make it easier for people to cross the road. Look, there's one here.'

'How do you know so much about the place?' she asked.

'I did some work on here.'

'What sort of work?' A tour guide in the summer holidays when he was a student, perhaps?

His answer surprised her. 'I wrote a couple of articles about the medicine of Pompeii. This place has fascinated me right from when I was a tiny child and came here with my nanny.'

Not with his mother, she noticed. 'Did you ever think about becoming an archaeologist?'

He nodded. 'But, like you, I wanted to make

people better. I had to make the choice between studying medicine and studying archaeology. I think I made the right choice: this way I get the best of both worlds, with a job I love and a place to escape.'

'Have your papers been trans—?'

Eleanor didn't get the chance to finish asking her question, because they heard a cry and saw a man in front of them stagger and lean against the wall, clutching his stomach with one hand and gripping the wall with the other.

'*C'è un problema?*' Orlando asked.

'Not…speak…Italian,' the man gasped. 'American.'

Orlando switched to English. 'What's wrong?'

'Feel dizzy. Sick. Stomach hurts.' The man dragged in a breath. 'Can't see properly.'

'Do you have any pain anywhere, apart from your stomach?' Eleanor asked.

'My head,' he croaked.

Eleanor checked his pulse: it was racing and thumping. His forehead was hot, even allowing for the weather—and it was dry rather than sweaty.

She exchanged a glance with Orlando.

He mouthed, 'Heatstroke?'

It wasn't something she saw much of in England—except in a rare heatwave—but the symptoms certainly seemed like it. They needed to get the man out of the sun and start to cool him down—now. Gently, she took the tourist's arm. 'We're both doctors. Let's get you into the shade so we can have a look at you.' She led him into a cool, quiet area where he could sit down.

'Are you on your own or with a group of people?' Orlando asked.

'MedAm tours,' he said. 'I lost my party. Stopped to look at something. They'd gone.'

'I'll go and find your guide,' Orlando said. 'And get a medical kit. I didn't put mine in the car today but the office here should have something.' He took a handkerchief from his pocket—clean, folded and uncrumpled—and handed it to Eleanor, along with his bottle of water. 'Eleanor's an emergency doctor, so I'm leaving you in good hands,' he said gently. 'Don't worry. We'll get help for you.'

'What's your name?' Eleanor asked.

'Jed Baynes.'

'Pleased to meet you, Jed. I'm Eleanor Forrest.'

"I'm not drunk,' Jed said to Eleanor when

Orlando had left. 'Don't even drink. But my head *hurts*. Like a killer hangover.'

She noticed he wasn't wearing a hat. And he didn't appear to be carrying any water with him. 'Have you been in the sun long?' she asked.

'No, just since first thing this morning.'

She glanced at her watch. It was nearly half past twelve, so he'd probably been out in the sun for at least three hours. And right now it was the hottest part of the day. 'No hat?'

'Forgot it. Wanted to see the ruins.' He grimaced. 'Didn't think.'

'Have you stopped for a drink?'

'No.'

And in this heat he'd be dehydrated even before he felt thirsty. Not good. 'OK. I think you've just been in the sun too long. You need some water.' She unscrewed the lid from her water bottle, wiped the neck with Orlando's handkerchief and handed it to Jed. 'Take a sip. Not lots of gulps, or you'll bring it back up again—just take it nice and slowly. One sip at a time.' She opened Orlando's water and dampened the handkerchief with it, then gently dabbed it across Jed's face. 'We need to cool you down a bit,' she said softly. At least he was wearing loose shorts and a shirt, so his clothing wasn't going to make things worse. 'Have you ever had anything like this before?'

'No.'

'When Dr de Luca's back, hopefully he'll have a thermometer with him. I think you've got a temperature—and we might need to get you to hospital to help you cool down.'

'I don't want to make a fuss!'

'It's no trouble,' she reassured him, and dampened the handkerchief again. A quick glance showed her that Jed's pupils weren't dilated, so hopefully they'd caught him before his condition spiralled out of control.

Within a few minutes Orlando had returned with a medical kit. 'They're getting in touch with the tour leader on his mobile phone. I told them exactly where to find us.' He handed Eleanor the thermometer.

'Would you mind just popping this under your tongue for me?' Eleanor wiped the thermometer, then handed it to Jed. As soon as it beeped, she checked the electronic reading. 'Your temperature's very high—almost forty-one.'

Orlando said in low tones, 'If you've been cooling him down since I left you, then I'm really not happy. It's still way too high. He could end up having a fit.' He sat down on the other side of Jed and took his hand. 'Are you taking any medication?'

'My blood pressure's a bit high,' Jed said. 'I'm on tablets for it.'

'Diuretics—water tablets?' Orlando asked.

'That's right.'

'And you've been taking them regularly?'

'Just like the doctor ordered.'

'That's really good, Jed,' Eleanor said, 'but the tablets you've been taking are a type that makes you more susceptible to heatstroke.'

'So we'd be much happier if we get you to hospital and get you checked over—your blood pressure needs checking, too. I'll call the ambulance now,' Orlando said.

Jed looked embarrassed. 'I'll be all right. Just need to sit in the shade. I don't want to make a fuss.'

Eleanor stroked his hand. 'You're not making a fuss—but you're not used to this kind of heat. Being English, neither am I. If you don't sit down now and cool down properly, you could end up being very ill indeed. You might even collapse and fall unconscious—and that would make even more of a fuss, wouldn't it?'

Orlando spoke rapid Italian into his mobile phone. Eleanor caught the words *'febbre'*, *'mal di testa'* and *'il colpo di sole'* and guessed that Orlando was giving a list of Jed's symptoms and diagnosis.

Jed's hand tightened around Eleanor's. 'But I can't go to hospital. I don't speak Italian. I won't know what they're saying.' He swallowed hard. 'And they won't understand me.'

Orlando exchanged a glance with Eleanor as he ended his call. 'Don't worry, Jed. We'll come with you. I'll translate,' he said.

Jed frowned. 'But I'm spoiling your honeymoon.'

Eleanor blinked. 'Um, we're not married.'

Jed flushed. 'I'm sorry. The way you look at each other…I thought you were…'

'Confusion's all part of heatstroke,' Orlando said to Eleanor in low tones.

True. But they had been holding hands when they'd first gone to Jed's rescue. And Eleanor knew exactly what Jed meant: she and Orlando had been looking at each other like that since the moment they'd met on the plane.

Hot.

Wanting.

Like lovers.

Except they weren't.

Yet. The word shimmered into her mind. The attraction was there. Mutual. They were both single. Would they…?

'The ambulance will be here in about ten minutes,' Orlando said. 'You go in the ambulance with Jed, Eleanor. I'll follow in my car.'

'You speak Italian?' Jed asked her hopefully.

'A little.' Not enough to translate for him in the ambulance. 'Surely it'd make more sense for you to go in the ambulance and translate?' she asked Orlando.

Orlando shook his head. 'You don't know the way to the hospital—and I'd hate you to get lost.'

She laughed. 'Listen to him, Jed. He's got this flash Italian sports car. Sounds to me like he doesn't want me to drive it.'

Orlando snorted. 'In that case, when we've got Jed settled at the hospital, you can drive us home.'

Eleanor backtracked fast. 'I was teasing.'

'No, it was a definite challenge. Don't you think, Jed?'

Jed tried to smile, but he was clearly in pain. Eleanor encouraged him to take small sips of water. 'Not long now, honey.'

'*Cos'è?*' A man came hurrying towards them. 'Mr Baynes? What's happened?'

Orlando explained quickly while Eleanor continued trying to cool Jed down; by the time Orlando had finished explaining, the paramedics had arrived. He went through the handover, then said to Eleanor, 'I've given them a patient history. I told them you're an English emergency specialist who doesn't speak much Italian, but you will know what they are doing and will help to explain to Jed.'

'I will get in touch with your family, Mr Baynes, and tell them what's happening,' the tour leader said, 'and then I will get someone to take over from me and I will join you at the hospital.'

Eleanor persuaded Jed to allow the paramedics to carry him to the ambulance—it would be quicker and avoid him rushing and making the heatstroke worse. But Orlando's grim prediction came true in the ambulance when Jed went into convulsions.

The paramedics immediately gave him diazepam, to control the fitting, and an oxygen mask.

'At the moment your body's too hot and it's making you have a fit,' she explained to Jed, holding his hand. 'They've given you some drugs to stop you having a fit. And the oxygen's to help you breathe more easily.' Diazepam could depress respiration, but Jed was worried enough: he didn't need something else to panic about.

'When you get to hospital, they'll cool you down properly,' she explained. 'They'll probably spray you with tepid water and blow fans over you.' Immersion in cool water wasn't an option in this case, as he'd already had a fit and the potential resuscitation problems made it unworkable. 'They might put cool packs in your armpits, over your neck and scalp, and in your groin area.'

Jed looked askance and lifted the mask from his face. 'My groin?'

'Put this back because you need the oxygen right now,' she said quietly, helping him settle the mask back in place. 'The packs will help to cool you more quickly. It's standard treatment, so try not to worry. They might give you some more drugs to stop you having another fit or feeling sick, and they'll take some blood so they can check the chemicals in your blood are all as they should be and give you something to help if they're not.'

When they got to the emergency department, Orlando was already there.

'You drive like a maniac,' she said. 'I think we should bet on him to win the next Grand Prix, Jed.'

Orlando just laughed. 'How are you feeling, Jed?' he asked.

'Terrible.'

'You'll be feeling much better soon,' Orlando promised.

Orlando translated everything that the medics were doing for Jed's benefit, and by the time the MedAm tour leader arrived, Jed's condition had stabilised enough for them to be happy to leave him with the tour leader.

'You take care. And enjoy the rest of your holiday,' Orlando said, patting Jed's shoulder.

Jed nodded. 'Thank you. I don't know how to repay you for the way you looked after me.'

Orlando shrugged. 'We're doctors. This is what we do. Just have good memories of my country—that will be enough for me.'

Eleanor followed Orlando into the car park. He leaned against his car door and took the keys from his pocket. 'So. I drive like a maniac, do I?'

She rubbed a hand against her face. 'No, just a bit faster than I'm used to.'

'A maniac, you said.' He raised an eyebrow. 'Right. Let's see what you can do.' He tossed the keys towards her.

She caught them automatically—and then froze. 'Orlando, I can't do this. I'm not insured.'

'Under the terms of my insurance, anyone over the age of twenty-five can drive, with my permission.' His eyes sparkled. 'And I give you my permission, Eleanor.'

'I've never driven a left-hand-drive car before.'

'So?' He spread his hands. 'You're perfectly capable. You can do anything you want to, if you try.'

'You're really going to let me drive your car?'

'Uh-huh.' He smiled at her. 'We've already established that we make a good team. Tell you what, you drive, I'll direct you, and we'll stop somewhere for a late lunch.'

She'd get to drive this gorgeous car with the top down and music playing and the sunlight sparkling on the sea. Amazing.

And then her elation faded as she took in what he'd said. 'You're going to make me drive through Naples?'

'When you're used to the car, maybe. The traffic here's even crazier than it is in London. For now, we'll take the quieter roads. Relax. Enjoy.' He gestured to the car. 'And I'm hungry. So can you, please, get in and drive?'

She climbed into the driver's side and put the key into the ignition. Orlando put the roof down again, and stretched his arm along the back of her seat. Close enough to touch her.

But that was fine. She'd promised herself she'd stop fussing and planning and let things just happen as they would.

He directed her out of the hospital car park and along the coast road. When they were on the open road, he switched programmes on his MP3 player; she recognised the singer as Andrea

Bocelli. By the third song Orlando was singing along—and he had a beautiful voice, a rich tenor. Better still, he sang in tune.

Good music, good company, good weather, and a fast car that responded perfectly to her. She couldn't remember when she'd last enjoyed herself this much.

'My singing is that bad?' Orlando asked.

She frowned. 'No, it's fine. Why do you ask?'

'You had a pained expression on your face. Why?'

She shrugged. 'Nothing, really.'

'Tell me,' he invited.

Well, he'd asked. She may as well tell him. 'It's the first time I can remember enjoying myself like this for a long, long time.'

His fingers brushed against the nape of her neck. 'Then stop thinking about it, *tesoro*, and enjoy. Because it's only going to get better.'

CHAPTER FIVE

ORLANDO directed Eleanor down a narrow road on the side of a cliff, full of hairpin bends; he knew that she was having to concentrate on the drive and that the sheer drop on her right-hand side was definitely occupying her, but he thought she'd agree that their destination was worth it.

'Next turn on the right,' he said, directing her into a car park.

She pulled up and gazed at the view over the sea. 'Wow. That's stunning.'

'One of my favourite places,' he said. 'And the food's even better than the view.'

It was only a few minutes before they were seated in a shady spot overlooking the sea, with hunks of good bread, a bowl of green salad and two steaming plates of monkfish in a garlicky tomato sauce.

'This has to be the best fish I've ever eaten,' Eleanor said. 'And the best sauce.'

'It's *ragù Napoletana*. Of course it's the best,' he said with a grin.

'Thank you.'

'My pleasure. And I'm so glad you're not one of these women who only eats a tiny morsel and says she couldn't possibly manage any more.'

'Not when the food's this good.'

When they'd mopped the last of the sauce from their plates, she opted for a *lattè* rather than pudding. Then she was aware of his expression.

'What?'

'How can you possibly drink *lattè* after a meal?'

She smiled. 'Because I prefer *lattès* to the lukewarm, incredibly strong stuff you drink.'

'It's the way we drink coffee here.'

'And I'm a tourist,' she reminded him.

He laughed. 'Ah. I forgot. Because you look so Italian. You *are* Italian.'

'Half Italian, half English,' she corrected him. 'And I'll be going halves with you on the bill for lunch.'

Not if he could help it. He'd pay for it without telling her—and then, when the waitress told her that Dottore de Luca had already settled the bill, he had a good excuse to have lunch with her again later in the week. A little underhand, perhaps, but he wanted to spend time with her, and she had this ridiculous idea about imposing on people so she'd probably refuse a second invitation to lunch. Doing it this way neatly circumvented the problem.

But then she went quiet on him. Was she worried about her father—or was there more to it than that? Why was a woman as lovely as Eleanor Forrest—kind, beautiful, funny and clever—alone? And why was she so adamant about paying her way for things, about not being beholden to anyone?

He placed his hand over hers and rubbed his thumb over the back of her hand. Lord, her skin was soft. Touching her made his blood fizz through his veins; it made him want to touch her more intimately. Much more intimately.

'Penny for them?' he asked.

'I'm fine.'

'That's not what your eyes are saying. If I promise you the protection of the Hippocratic oath...?' He squeezed her hand gently. 'Talk to me, *bella mia*. Tell me why you're sad. It's not just concern about your father, is it?'

'No. I was thinking about the choices we make. If my mother had chosen differently, I might have grown up around here.'

He was pretty sure there was more to it than that. So he waited. And finally she filled the silence. 'I made a really bad choice last year.'

'How?' he prompted softly.

'I fell in love. With someone at work. I thought he was in love with me.'

From the expression on her face, she'd clearly been wrong.

'We were going to move in together, but we hadn't quite sorted it out. He bought me an engagement ring—said it was only a cheap one because he had to support his mum since she'd lost her job. She'd supported him through med school so he thought it was his turn to support her.'

The man was obviously a confidence trickster. One who knew exactly which buttons to press. Eleanor believed in sharing and fairness and family. Those words would've gone straight to her heart.

'I didn't mind. Jewellery doesn't bother me

and I'd rather be with someone who cared about his family than someone who spent loads of money on fripperies.'

Exactly as he'd guessed. 'So what happened? His family came between you?'

Her face tightened. 'Hardly. He wasn't supporting his mother.'

'So what was he doing with the money? He'd invested badly? Addicted to online poker games?' No, Eleanor wouldn't be hard on someone who'd made a mistake. It had to be more serious than that. 'He had a drug habit?'

She shook her head. 'He was supporting someone. Except she was his girlfriend.'

'The man you loved cheated on you?'

She dragged in a breath. 'She didn't work at the hospital so he'd managed to keep her secret. But she'd finally had enough of him messing about and promising her things he wouldn't deliver. Especially as she was three months into her pregnancy.'

'Oh, no. The...' He switched to Italian, not wanting to offend her but needing to vent his disgust. 'What happened?'

'She confronted me.' Eleanor closed her eyes.

'Luckily it was *before* I'd signed the paperwork to open a joint bank account with him. So if he'd been planning to transfer my funds, it didn't happen.'

'Ellie, I'm so sorry.' His hand rested over hers again, squeezed it comfortingly. 'He preyed on you when you were vulnerable.'

'My mum was my only family after Dad died. So when she was diagnosed with cancer—with secondaries—I was...' She swallowed hard. 'Jeremy was just *there*. He let me lean on him. I'd known him vaguely for a while, danced with him at parties and what have you. I'd heard rumours that he was a bit ambitious, but he was always perfectly charming when he came to the department to discuss a patient. And he was, um, rather nice-looking.'

Was that white-hot flare at the base of his spine *jealousy*? Orlando was too shocked to say anything.

Luckily she seemed to misread his silence, as if he'd accused her of being shallow. 'It wasn't just me. Most of the female staff really fancied him. And when he asked me out I was... I dunno. Flattered. Glad to have something else to think about other than the fact that my mum was dying.'

And clearly she'd been twice as disillusioned when she'd found out the truth—that the man she'd loved hadn't loved her. The bastard had tried to take advantage of her instead. Worse, he'd done it when he'd been committed elsewhere.

'I thought Jeremy loved me. I thought I loved him,' she said softly. 'I thought he was the one.'

He laced his fingers through hers. 'Maybe this "The One" thing is a myth. Love doesn't really exist like that.'

'How do you mean?'

He stared out to sea. 'My mother is always searching for The One. And she never finds him. She's been divorced five times. Is it really worth all the pain and disappointment?'

She frowned. 'So what are you saying? That people shouldn't even bother looking?'

'Just that they shouldn't be blinded by an impossible ideal when they choose their partner.'

'You mean, have an arranged marriage?'

'Maybe.' He formulated the words carefully. 'If you're good friends, that's an excellent basis for a relationship. It means you'll never be disappointed in each other. You'll have something to keep you together when the first flush of passion fades.'

Eleanor shook her head. 'There's more to love than just friendship or sex.'

He wished she hadn't used that particular word. Because right now he could imagine Eleanor lying in the grass in a lemon grove, giving him that sensual smile as he slowly, slowly stroked the clothes from her body and explored her skin with his mouth.

'My parents were happy,' she continued. 'They loved each other. And my best friend's happily married.'

'So how do you know when you find this "love", then?' Orlando asked.

She shrugged. 'I don't know. I assume you meet someone and you know you want to be with them for the rest of your life. You want to wake up with them. You want to go to sleep in their arms.'

'That's just sexual attraction,' Orlando corrected.

'That,' she said, shaking her head in apparent disbelief, 'is outrageously cynical.'

'Realistic,' he countered. 'And sexual attraction

wears off. When it's over, what do you have left? Unless, as I said, you're friends to start with.'

'So you'd marry someone who was a friend?'

'If I liked them enough. If I thought we'd make a good life together.'

She removed her hand from his, propped her elbows on the table and rested her chin on her linked hands. 'There's a flaw in your argument, you know. A huge one.'

'Which is?'

'You're not actually married,' she pointed out.

'Because I'm picky.'

'More like, if you explained your views on marriage to any woman you were thinking of asking to marry you, she'd shove you in the nearest puddle and tell you what to do with your ring.'

'I've never explained it to anyone before.' He'd never wanted to get married. His affairs had always been for mutual pleasure and he'd made it clear right from the start, so nobody had got hurt. 'I probably didn't make a good job of explaining it just now.'

A corner of her mouth quirked. 'I do hope you're not going to claim that your English was too poor for you to explain your theory to me.'

'When I lived in England for a couple of years? Hardly. I might miss a few of the more obscure idioms, but...' He smiled back at her. 'No, I just phrased it badly. What I mean is that these people who claim they've found The One are just infatuated. They have this grand idea of what love should be and they're determined to find it. They're expecting rainbows and fireworks and a thousand balloons to float through the sky every time they kiss—and that really doesn't last for ever. If they're not good friends with their lover to start with, once the infatuation wears off there's nothing left to keep them together. No shared interests, no jointly held views on life, no real bond.'

'So how do you explain my parents? They were married for over twenty years. They really believed in "till death us do part".'

'Maybe they were lucky.' He shrugged. 'Maybe the infatuation didn't wear off.'

'They loved each other, Orlando.' She stared at him. 'I can't believe you're such a cynic. You're *Italian*. And Italians are meant to be the most romantic race on earth. Look at Romeo and Juliet.'

'Who didn't live happily ever after, if you remember,' he pointed out.

'But they loved each other.'

'So did Dante's Paolo and Francesca. And Manzoni's Renzo and Lucia. And Petrarca and whatever the woman's name was that he wrote all those sonnets to.' He spread his hands. 'They're *fictional*, Eleanor. Just like love. A figment of a poet's imagination.'

'So you're saying you don't believe in love?'

'I believe in friendship. And in sexual attraction. But love...that's a con.'

She raised an eyebrow. 'Some people believe men and women can't be friends. That sex always gets in the way.'

'Not true. We're friends, aren't we? Or on our way to becoming friends.'

'Maybe.'

She didn't tackle the other question, he noticed. About sexual attraction.

He was definitely attracted to Eleanor. Had been, right from the first time he'd seen her. That mouth was just made for kissing. He wanted to slide his fingers through her short dark hair, feel just how silky and soft it was. Wanted to stroke her skin until she was boneless with pleasure.

And he liked her, too. He liked her no-nonsense practicality. He liked the warmth of her smile. And when they'd held hands this morning in Pompeii, he'd been close to kissing her. Probably would have kissed her under a lemon tree overlooking the sea—had they not ended up rescuing a fellow tourist.

He was pretty sure the attraction was mutual. There was heat in her dark eyes when she looked at him. He'd felt the pulse throbbing when he'd linked his fingers through hers—a little too hard, a little too fast.

But love?

Who the hell knew what love was, anyway?

'So how long are you planning to stay in Italy?' he asked.

'A few days. Maybe a couple of weeks. Enough to get to know Bartolomeo a little better.'

'And then you're going back to England—back to the hospital to work in the emergency department?'

She took a sip of her *lattè*. 'Probably. Though right now I'm not sure if I want to go back to emergency medicine.'

'Because you'll have to face this Jeremy?'

'It's been a bit hideous at work,' she admitted. 'He's a surgeon, so we don't exactly work together—but obviously everyone knows what happened, and I've really hated being pitied by my colleagues. Poor Ellie, who got taken for a ride. Jeremy's baby's due in a couple of weeks so the sympathy's been a bit choking lately. But something else will knock me off the hospital grapevine soon enough. By the time I get back, hopefully everyone will have forgotten about it.'

'So if it's not embarrassment, why don't you want to go back?'

She sighed. 'What you said about wanting to see your patients grow up—sometimes I think that's what I want, too. Or maybe it's because I've lost my family and I miss them and I want to get that feeling back—and working in family medicine would give me that feeling again. I don't know. Right now I don't trust my judgement in anything except a clinical situation.'

He knew he was storing up trouble, but he couldn't help himself. 'I have a suggestion for you.'

'What?'

'I assume you'd like to see a lot of Bartolomeo, as he's your only blood family now.'

She nodded. 'But I can't keep flying between UK and Italy.'

'Why don't you stay out here for a while? Talk to your boss, take a sabbatical. And if money's a problem, you're a qualified doctor—we could do with a hand in our practice.'

'But I'm qualified in England.'

'A qualification that is valid here, too.'

She shook her head. 'I'm hospital-trained. I haven't done a GP rotation. And I haven't got the right paperwork.'

He shrugged. 'We can work around it. And the paperwork will be easy enough to sort out.'

'My Italian isn't good enough to deal with patients.'

'That,' he said, 'is temporary. And you can always start by helping expats and tourists—look at today. Your language skills and your medical skills were perfect. You really helped Jed.'

'You had to do the handover. I couldn't have told the paramedics what was going on.'

'It's a matter of vocabulary. You're bright: you'll pick up the language quickly.' He paused. Now this would definitely mean they'd have to spend time together. 'I can teach you. Test you on your vocabulary, if you like.'

She frowned. 'Why? Why me?'

'Why not you? I like you, Eleanor. I've seen the way you work in an emergency—twice now. You're good with people and I think you'd be an excellent family doctor. Think about it. You could spend the summer in Italy. Have the chance to see if this is the kind of medicine you want to do, without taking any risks. And take the opportunity to get to know Bartolomeo.' And get to know me, he added silently. See if this thing between us is real. See if you're right and I'm wrong.

She rubbed a hand across her face. 'I could talk to my boss. See if I can take some time off. Though I don't want to live in a hotel.'

'You don't have to.' He just about stopped himself from offering her a room at his place. He didn't want to rush her, he wanted them to get to know each other. Properly. Living together would only get in the way. 'I can help you find an apartment.'

'I'll think about it.'

'It's an open offer.' He finished his espresso.

'Would you like another coffee—well, a fat-laden excuse for coffee, in your case?'

She laughed. 'Another *lattè* would be lovely. Thank you.' Her eyes crinkled at the corners. '*Grazie*, Orlando.'

Lord, he loved it when she spoke his language. And how he'd like to hear her say—

No. He really shouldn't rush her. Especially because she was so vulnerable right now. She'd already been hurt badly. He wasn't going to make it worse by pushing her into something she wasn't ready for. 'I'll go and order it.'

He paid the bill at the same time. And just as he'd expected, Eleanor was annoyed about it when she found out.

'You're not under any obligation to me,' he reminded her. 'Lunch was my idea.'

She folded her arms. 'You know how I feel about paying my way.'

'If it makes you feel better, you can buy me lunch some other time.' He kept the suggestion very light, very casual. 'I have a clinic this evening, so I'd better drive us back.' He opened the passenger door for her. What he really wanted to do was to kiss her. But if he pushed her too hard, too fast, he knew she'd walk away. She needed time to think. And he wanted her to stay in Italy for a while.

'Are you seeing Bartolomeo tomorrow?' he asked when he parked outside the hotel.

'We haven't made any arrangements.'

'Then, unless you have anything pressing to do, you're very welcome to shadow me for the day. See how our practice works. And if you like what you see, and your boss will let you have a sabbatical out here, I can help you sort out the paperwork later in the week.'

Again, he waited, knowing that it had to be her decision.

Finally, she nodded. 'Thank you, Orlando. I'd like that.'

'Then I will see you tomorrow,' he said. 'Unless you call me to tell me you're busy, I'll pick you up at eight. Will that give you enough time for breakfast?'

She nodded. 'It doesn't take that long to drink coffee and eat toast.'

He'd missed an opportunity there: he should've suggested taking her to a *caffè* overlooking the sea for breakfast—coffee and brioches, maybe some fruit. But maybe he was being greedy. At least she'd agreed to spend the day with him. '*A domani*. See you tomorrow.'

'See you tomorrow,' she echoed.

On impulse, he leaned forward and kissed her on the cheek. His lips actually tingled at the contact, and it took all his self-control not to yank her into his arms and kiss her properly. On the mouth.

CHAPTER SIX

THE next morning, Orlando was already waiting for Eleanor in the hotel foyer. He was dressed formally in a suit and tie, and he was the subject of more than a few nudges and glances and whispers. Again, he seemed oblivious of the female interest in him; he merely stood up when he saw Eleanor and gave her a tiny bow.

She noticed the disappointment on the faces around them when they realised he was indeed waiting for someone. Ha. They'd be even more disappointed if they found out he didn't believe in love. Whereas it suited her fine.

'Sorry—am I late?' she asked.

'No.' His eyes crinkled at the corners. 'I'm early. Ready?'

'Yes. And thank you for doing this, Orlando. I appreciate it.'

'Believe me, we'll appreciate you just as much

if you decide to join us for the summer,' he told her. 'We're a busy practice.'

They took the metro to his consulting rooms. 'Right. I'll introduce you to everyone and show you where everything is,' he said.

'You're sure your partner in the practice doesn't mind?'

'Partners,' he said. 'They're looking forward to meeting you. Though they'll drive you mad because they'll try to practise their English on you.'

'You're the senior partner?' she asked.

'No. We're all equals. Actually, we're more or less the same age. Alessandro's married to Serafina, our practice nurse, and Giacomo's getting married in September.' He grimaced. 'So they will also drive you mad, trying to pair you off with me.'

'Why would they try to do that?'

He rubbed a hand across his face. 'Because they're a little *pazzo*. Crazy. They're in love and think everyone else should be, too.'

She laughed. 'You mean, you haven't told them your theory?'

'They don't believe me. They can't pair me off with a patient because it's unethical, our receptionist Chiara is old enough to be my mother, and I've resisted every single one of the little dinner parties they hold to introduce me to a suitable woman who will reform me.' He rolled his eyes. 'You're in the right age group—so in their eyes you'll be a suitable woman.'

'All cats being grey in the dark, you mean?'

He looked quizzically at her. 'That's not a phrase I'm familiar with.'

'Any port in a storm.'

'Ha.' He smiled and ruffled her hair. 'I'm almost tempted to tease them and... No. That wouldn't be fair to you. But if they go on about it, I'll kiss you in front of them and you can pretend to faint. Then they'll leave us alone and we can get on with our work.'

She coughed. 'Orlando, you're something else.'

'I think I'll take that as a compliment.' He smiled. 'Welcome to our practice, Dottoressa Forrest.'

Alessandro and Giacomo were both charming. Serafina looked as angelic as her name; she glanced at Eleanor and then Orlando, and broke into a wide smile before whispering something to her husband. And Chiara rolled her eyes, shooed them all away and gave Eleanor a cup of coffee before showing her around the building and making sure that she was comfortable.

It felt, Eleanor thought with a pang, like being part of a big, noisy family. They were clearly close to each other—behind the banter and the teasing she could tell that they all cared deeply about each other.

Orlando shepherded her through to his consulting room for the beginning of morning surgery; when each patient arrived, he introduced them to Eleanor and asked their permission for her to remain during the consultation, explaining that she might be staying to join the practice. And although Eleanor couldn't follow all the conversations, she picked up odd words during the consultation that, coupled with the kind of tests he did, made her realise exactly what each medical problem was.

She noticed that Orlando was particularly good with the children who came to see him. He was careful in the way he conducted the hearing test and then checked inside one little boy's ears with the otoscope: a case of glue ear, she guessed, because Orlando's gestures when he spoke to the mother showed that the little boy's hearing was slightly better on the right side and it'd be easier for the little boy if people who talked to him came down to his level and kept sentences short and simple. He made the little boy laugh by doing magic tricks and making a coin appear from behind his ear, followed up with a sticker with a smiley face saying *'Coraggioso'*—the equivalent of the 'I was *this* brave' stickers she gave out at the emergency department.

She'd just bet he'd been the most popular doctor on his ward when he'd worked in paediatrics, charming the parents as well as the patients. The little girl who came in wheezing left with a smile as well as an inhaler to help her asthma. And Eleanor could just imagine him with a little girl of his own, cuddling her on his lap and telling her stories. A little girl with long curly hair, just as Eleanor herself had once been…

Oh, lord. Now, there was a fantasy she really ought to stop right now. Constance Firth had fallen in love with a Neapolitan man and it had all gone pear-shaped. Eleanor wasn't about to follow in her mother's footsteps. She and Orlando were friends. Nothing more. And marriage and children really weren't on the agenda for her anyway.

During a coffee-break, Serafina made a point of looking at Eleanor's left hand. She said something in Italian to Alessandro, who smiled and agreed.

Orlando groaned. 'Apart from the fact that it's really rude to speak only Italian when Eleanor can't follow, will you two, please, stop it? We're just friends.'

'I've heard that one before,' Giacomo said with a grin. 'Just *good* friends, is it?'

'Right. That's it.' Orlando marched over to Eleanor, grabbed her hand, yanked her into his arms, bent her over backwards and kissed her.

It was meant to be a kiss for show. They'd even discussed it beforehand.

But he hadn't expected this.

Time stopped and the room dissolved. There was nobody else there, just the two of them. Kissing. For real. Because her hands had slid into his hair, and as he nibbled at her lower lip her mouth opened, letting him deepen the kiss. He could hear the blood roaring in his ears and he felt as if he were falling very slowly from a very great height.

When Orlando broke the kiss, he was disorientated at first. All he could focus on was Eleanor. Her pupils were huge and her mouth looked as if she'd just been very thoroughly kissed.

Well, she had.

Oh, hell. That wasn't meant to happen. She'd run a mile if she had any idea of the crazy thoughts whirling through his mind. Crazy thoughts, like picking her up, carrying her into his office, locking the door behind them and continuing from where they'd just left off.

And heaven only knew what his colleagues were thinking after witnessing that.

His *colleagues*.

Um.

Head still swimming, he lifted his chin and raised an eyebrow at Alessandro, Giacomo and Serafina, who were staring at them in apparent disbelief. 'Let that,' he said in a voice that didn't really sound to him like his own, 'be an end to the gossip.'

'*Porca miseria!*' Serafina fanned herself. 'No more questions. I promise. Alessandro, why don't you kiss me like that?' she demanded.

'In public, you mean? Because, *mia innamorata*, it would not be good for the blood pressure of our patients. Or our colleagues,' Alessandro teased, taking her hand and kissing the backs of her fingers.

Giacomo assumed an angelic posture. 'I'm saying nothing.' But his smile said it all for him. *You've found The One.*

Ridiculous. It was a myth Orlando didn't subscribe to.

So why was adrenaline racing round his system like this?

Eleanor didn't remember anything more from the coffee-break, even though there was an empty cup of coffee in her hand, which she'd presumably drunk. The kiss had been for show—Orlando had even warned her before they'd left the car that his colleagues would drive them crazy and he'd probably have to kiss her to shut them up—but when he'd been supporting her, she hadn't been acting. At all. Her knees really *had* gone weak.

And she'd never reacted like that to anyone before. Not even Jeremy, and she'd thought she'd loved him. Now she knew it hadn't been love at all. Because what she felt for Orlando was so much stronger. One kiss, and her head was spinning.

This was mad. Completely mad. It couldn't possibly work out between them. Orlando was as damaged as she was—more so, in fact, because he didn't believe that love even existed. But, lord, the man could kiss.

'Are you all right, Eleanor?' Orlando asked when they were back in his consulting room. 'Sorry. Was I too rough with you?'

'No, it's not a problem.' Not quite the truth. But her brain wasn't quite working in synch with her mouth after that kiss. Worse, she wanted him to do it again. This time in private. When they wouldn't have to stop.

'You look a bit…'

Stunned? Shocked? Yeah, that was exactly how she felt. She hadn't expected that surge of emotion when he'd kissed her. Hadn't expected the world to melt away. Hadn't expected to find herself kissing him back.

'Maybe working together isn't such a good idea,' she said carefully.

Orlando's eyes widened. 'No, no, no.' He crossed his hands rapidly in front of him. 'That kiss was just to shut them up. For show. I did warn you it was the only way.'

Mmm. But she hadn't expected a kiss for show to be so—well—mind-blowing.

'Don't worry, I'm not going to pounce on you. You're perfectly safe.'

She should have been relieved. Instead, she felt disappointed.

When the last patient from the morning's surgery had left, Orlando finished writing up his notes.

'Time for lunch,' he said.

'Only if I pay. Seeing as you were sneaky about yesterday.'

He folded his arms. 'Hmm. You've been shadowing me today. Either I have to pay you for your work today—or you let me buy you lunch.'

'I haven't exactly done any work,' she protested.

'You will, this afternoon—we have house calls. And I'm starving.'

So am I, Eleanor thought. Though not for food.

'So, Dottoressa Forrest, are you going to let me buy you a ham and fontina *panini* and one of your touristy *lattès*?'

She could only nod.

Orlando led her through the maze of tiny streets, pointing out buildings of interest and the best *gelati* shop in Naples. They ended up at a little *caffè* where he ordered their lunch.

'So, what do you think of family medicine? Is it the sort of thing you'd like to practise?'

'Maybe. I can see why you enjoy it. And you're good with children.'

He smiled. 'I like children.'

So did he want any of his own? Was he looking to settle down and get married—to someone he considered a friend? And why should the idea of it make jealousy flicker in her stomach?

She concentrated on her coffee and the *panini*. But it didn't help. She kept finding herself glancing at Orlando—and catching him glancing at her.

The attraction was definitely mutual. But she was also aware that if she gave in to the impulse to suggest a mad affair and get it out of their systems, it would make life impossible. There was no way she could spend a summer here, working with him, when their affair ended—which it would. Because Orlando didn't believe in love or commitment.

After lunch, he took a detour to a florist's shop and purchased a bunch of bright summery flowers.

At her questioning look, he said, 'I've known

our next patient, Vittoria Moretti, since I was a child. She was my teacher at primary school.' He shrugged. 'Her family has moved to Rome. She's lonely. So when I call on her, I like to brighten her day a little.'

How typical of Orlando. A little kindness to make an old lady happy: he cared. He was a good man, whatever he claimed to think about love. Because he really did care.

'So tell me about our house calls. About Vittoria.'

'As I said, she taught me when I was tiny. She has an ulcerated leg.'

'Venous?' she asked.

He nodded. 'She had a clot in her leg.'

Typical presentation, Eleanor thought. She'd come across a few of them in the emergency department, when an elderly patient hadn't wanted to make a fuss and left it until the ulcer actually became painful or spread so much that someone noticed.

They took one of the funicular railways up one of the steeper hills, then he led them into a quiet street, rang the bell and then opened the front door. 'Signora Moretti? Vittoria?'

'Orlando! *Come va?*' She hobbled over to meet

them, then hugged him when he gave her the flowers and rattled off something in Italian that Eleanor couldn't follow before putting the flowers immediately in water.

'Vittoria, this is Eleanor Forrest. She's an English doctor who might join our practice for the summer,' Orlando explained in Italian.

'Elenora.' Vittoria pronounced the name the Italian way. 'My English…very little.'

'I'll translate,' Orlando said with a smile. He looked at Vittoria. 'May Eleanor examine your leg and treat you?'

'*Sì.*'

Gently, Eleanor removed the dressing and looked at the ulcer. The skin was darker and thicker around the area just above her ankle, and there was some swelling. 'Does it hurt at all?' she asked.

'She says it aches a bit and it's worse when she's been standing. But she hates sitting around and doing nothing,' Orlando translated.

Eleanor knew the type. The kind of elderly lady who liked to keep busy and tended to look about twenty years younger than she really was, because she kept active. 'Tell her it's a good idea to keep up gentle exercise,' she said, 'but emphasise the "gentle". Definitely no climbing these hills. And she needs to rest every so often and put her leg up on a cushion—if she keeps her leg higher than her hip, gravity will help pull the blood in the right direction, towards the heart. That will reduce the pressure of blood in her leg veins, and ease the swelling.'

Orlando translated, then laughed. 'She says she's not going to sit with her leg up on a cushion all day. She's far too busy.'

Eleanor smiled. 'Three or four times a day,' she said, 'for half an hour at a time. Tell her to lie on the sofa and put her foot on a couple of pillows.' She glanced at the bookshelves. 'It's a good excuse to read. Doctor's orders. But, yes, if she keeps moving about the rest of the time, it will help her leg heal.'

'*Bene,*' Vittoria said when Orlando had explained.

Eleanor gently cleaned the ulcer; it was at the earliest stage, when it was still moist and there was a lot of pus, so she took a non-adhesive absorbent dressing from Orlando's bag. 'We need to change the dressing daily until the ulcer has healed and dried.'

Vittoria clearly caught the word 'daily', and indicated that she didn't want a fuss.

'Tell her if we don't do that, the ulcer will take a lot longer to heal. But if we change the dressing daily and she wears elastic bandages, it will speed the healing.'

'You've done this before, haven't you?' Orlando asked.

'My speciality when I was a house officer,' she said. 'Geriatric medicine. I'm good at checking for diabetic foot, too.'

Deftly, she started applying elastic bandages over the dressing. 'Tell Vittoria it's not meant to hurt—if she feels any pain, I need to know right now because it means the compression's too tight and it will affect her circulation.'

'She says it's fine,' Orlando translated.

'Good.' She pursed her lips in frustration. 'I hate having to ask you to speak for me. It's wrong. I should be able to talk to my patient myself. Reassure her, listen to her, answer any questions she might have and second-guess what she's not asking me.'

Orlando smiled at her. 'You're a good doctor, Eleanor.'

'Not right now, I'm not. Can you tell Vittoria that she'll feel more pressure at the ankle and less towards the knee? And explain that this is to help counteract the raised pressure in the leg veins.' The pressure that had caused the problem in the first place.

When she'd put the third layer of bandages on, she checked that Vittoria could still move her ankle around. '*Più dolore*, um, *pede*?' she said to Vittoria, pointing to her foot, and mimed telephoning before pointing to herself.

'*Piede,*' Vittoria corrected with a smile, patting her hand. '*Bene.*'

'*Febbre,*' Eleanor said, remembering what Orlando had said about Jed's sunstroke, and mimed the phone again.

Vittoria laughed, and said something to Orlando.

'She says you're stubborn. And she likes the fact you're trying to speak Italian,' he informed Eleanor.

'Just confirm that if it starts to hurt more, or her foot feels hotter or colder or changes colour, she needs to call me straight away. I mean, call you,' she amended.

'Us,' Orlando said, 'and we will check her foot.' He quickly gave Vittoria Eleanor's instructions.

'And in the meantime, there's an exercise she can do sitting down.' She sat next to Vittoria and moved her foot in a circle, then up and down, then pointed to Vittoria. *'E lei?'*

Once she'd checked that Vittoria could do the exercise, she smiled. *'Una volta, due, ora?'*

Vittoria nodded, held up one finger and then a second, then mimed the minute hand going round her watch once.

Do it once or twice an hour. Exactly. *'Bene,'* Eleanor said, smiling.

Vittoria said something to Orlando, who nodded. 'She says you'll do,' he told Eleanor. 'You'll do just fine.'

And something in his eyes told her that he agreed.

CHAPTER SEVEN

ELEANOR rang her boss in England the next morning to see if she could arrange a sabbatical. When she'd explained the situation with Bartolomeo, Ian said immediately, 'Take as much time as you need. We can get locum cover for you here.'

'I feel as if I'm letting you down.'

'No, you're not. The last year's been pretty rough for you, and you're a marvel to have got through it as well as you have. Now you've got a chance to meet the family you never even knew existed, I think you should go for it. Spend some time with them.'

'There's a bit more to it than that,' she admitted. 'I've, um, had the offer of working over here. Temporarily.'

'And you want to do it?'

'Yes. So I'd better give you my resignation, hadn't I?'

'Not necessarily. You're a good registrar and we don't want to lose you,' Ian said. 'Anyway, working abroad would be good experience for you. Call it job enrichment, if you like. I'll sort out the admin side this end. If you need a reference, just let me know.'

Tears pricked her eyelids. 'I really appreciate this, Ian.' Especially the feeling that she belonged somewhere. That they'd keep her place open for her. Maybe her thoughts about leaving emergency medicine were just a knee-jerk reaction to the fact she missed her family. And maybe working in family medicine for a while would make her realise how much she loved her real job.

She heard the faint sound of a bleep on the other end of the phone. 'Ah, I'm needed in Resus. Gotta go. You take care, Ellie. Ring me if you need anything,' Ian said. 'And stay in touch. Let us know how you're getting on and when you're ready to come home.'

'Thanks, Ian.'

So now she could stay in Italy as long as she liked. Instead of the three weeks she'd planned, it could be the whole summer. Getting to know her father. Getting to know Orlando.

Even at her lowest point, she'd believed there would eventually be light at the end of the tunnel. Right now, it was blazing away like the Mediterranean sun itself.

For the next week, Eleanor spent her afternoons getting to know her father and her mornings shadowing Orlando in the surgery. The rest of the practice seemed to accept her as part of the team immediately: Serafina roped her in to help with the minor injuries clinic; Alessandro and Giacomo quizzed her about the way things were run in England and asked her opinion about setting up specialist clinics for their diabetic patients; Orlando talked about the possibility of setting up an expat clinic; and Chiara took Eleanor under her wing, making coffee exactly how Eleanor liked it without having to ask.

It was strange how she felt so at home in Naples—and so quickly.

And the more time she spent with Orlando, the more she liked him. He was funny, he was clever, and he cared.

But since that kiss in the surgery he'd kept an emotional distance between them. As if he was running scared.

She met Bartolomeo on the Friday for lunch in the city after the morning surgery ended, then spent the afternoon with him poring over his old family photographs, Bartolomeo explained who everyone was and told her little anecdotes that made her laugh. He also had some old ciné film that he'd had transferred to DVD format, and she had to swallow hard as she saw her mother at the age of twenty-one. Constance looked so beautiful, so vibrant.

'If only,' Eleanor said wistfully, 'the film had sound—so I could have heard Mum's voice just once more.'

'I know. It makes me feel that way, too,' Bartolomeo said, squeezing her hand. 'It reminds me of all the opportunities I missed. But I'm glad she had a happy life. I would have hated my Costanza to be sad.'

'Would you...? Could I, please, have a copy of the disc?' she asked. 'I'm more than happy to pay for it.'

'It will be my pleasure. And there's no need to

pay. I can do it for you myself.' He smiled at her. 'In fact, I can do it today. And this evening I will scan in the photographs for you and make you a CD of the stills.' He forestalled her protest with a lifted finger. 'It will amuse me to do it. And what's the point of having good computer equipment if you don't use it?'

Later that afternoon, when they were sitting on his terrace with coffee and pastries, Eleanor decided to tackle him about his health. Find out the truth. She'd hoped to be able to piece it together from the little bits she'd managed to get him to admit, but so far the diagnosis eluded her. Bartolomeo had avoided her gentle probing, so now she had to change tactics and ask him straight.

'So are you going to tell me what the problem is?' she asked. 'With your health, I mean?'

Bartolomeo waved a dismissive hand. 'Nothing is wrong, Eleanor.'

Obviously they were going to have to do this the hard way. 'I'm thirty, so that would make you...what...fifty-three?'

He nodded.

'And you're tired all the time.'

He shrugged. 'It's my age.'

No, it wasn't. 'And I suppose it's because of your age that you became breathless when we walking along the bay the other day?'

He smiled. 'Exactly so. I had a job where I sat down all day, every day. And even though I've sold the company now and I have time on my hands, I still don't exercise enough. I really should go to the gym.'

Eleanor scoffed. 'I'm a doctor, Bartolomeo. I add things together. Like the way you bruise easily—you're wearing short sleeves today so I can see the bruises.' Bruises in certain places that made her wonder if they'd been caused by a needle. 'And your gums were bleeding over lunch today.'

He made another dismissive gesture. 'Because the bread was a little too crusty.'

'It still shouldn't have made your gums bleed,' she said. 'And you're too young to be tired and breathless like this. I think your platelet count might be low. Are you going to tell me the truth about this, or do I have to nag you?'

He sighed. 'Your mother was sharp, like you. She noticed things. All right. The doctors say I have anaemia.'

Simple iron deficiency wouldn't have caused Bartolomeo's symptoms. There had to be more to it than that. 'What sort?'

'Aplastic.'

That explained a huge amount. The anaemia accounted for Bartolomeo's pallor—but aplastic anaemia was serious and couldn't be treated just by a course of iron tablets and changing his diet. The way he got tired so quickly and became short of breath was caused by low numbers of red cells in his blood. The way he bruised easily and his gums bled were due to low platelet levels, and she'd just bet, because his white cells weren't high enough either, that he picked up every cold and infection going. And it confirmed her suspicion that those bruises on his arms— bruises that seemed to appear between one day and the next—were due to transfusions into his arm. 'How long have you had it?'

He leaned back in his chair. 'Four months or so. Maybe a little longer before we found out what it was.'

In severe cases of aplastic anaemia, she knew that the chance of survival after six months of having the condition was less than fifty per cent.

So her guess was right. Bartolomeo was dying. He clearly knew he was on borrowed time, and that was why he'd tried to find Constance Firth. To make his peace with her before he died.

No. This wasn't fair. After thinking she was all alone in the world, Eleanor had found after all that she did have someone. Her biological father. In the few days they'd spent together she'd found that she liked him—liked him a lot—and she wanted to get to know him better.

But now she might not get the chance. Because the aplastic anaemia might take him from her. Way, way too quickly.

Well, she wasn't going to stand by and let it happen. There had to be something she could do.

'Do you know the cause?' she asked carefully.

'The consultant said there was no cause—it just happened.'

From what she could remember about the condition, it was an auto-immune reaction, caused when the body's immune system became confused and started to attack the body's own tissues; it damaged the bone marrow, and around two-thirds of cases had no known underlying cause. 'What treatment are you having?' she asked.

'Blood transfusions, antibiotics.'

They were standard treatments for the symptom of a low blood count, but they clearly weren't working well enough. 'What about a bone-marrow transplant?'

Bartolomeo closed his eyes. 'My sisters had the test to see if their tissues were compatible with mine. It seems that tissues aren't the same as blood type.'

She nodded. 'We inherit three antigens from each parent.' She drew a swift diagram on the back of a napkin, with a stick woman and a stick man; she added two blocks of three numbers underneath the woman and two blocks of three letters underneath the man. 'If you inherited 1, 2 and 3 from your mother and A, B and C from your father, that leaves 4, 5 and 6 and C, D and E that don't match your tissue type.' She drew a circle round each block of three antigens, then drew lines from each to show potential matches. 'You see? That gives you a one in four chance of the tissues matching.'

He smiled. 'Like a probability tree. You inherited my talent for maths, then.'

'Yes.' She smiled back, but her heart was heavy.

A one in four chance. Twenty-five per cent. The odds were too low. 'I take it they didn't match?'

'They match each other because they're twins—but, no, they don't match me. My consultant has put me on the waiting list for a donor, but...'

He didn't have to say any more. 'It's the same in my country. There aren't enough donors.' But when Bartolomeo had been put on the waiting list, the situation had been different. Then, he'd thought there was nobody in the family with his tissue type. Now he knew he had a child. One who would have inherited three of his antigens. Which meant a tissue match. 'We need to talk to Orlando.'

'Orlando?' Bartolomeo looked puzzled.

'I told you about him—the family doctor I'm working with right now.'

Bartolomeo's eyes narrowed. 'You haven't said that much about him. Or that you were working here, come to that. I thought you were here on holiday?'

'I met him on the plane on the way over,' Eleanor explained. 'We worked together to help a fellow passenger who'd had a heart attack. We became friends.'

'Friends?' Bartolomeo sounded suspicious.

She sighed. 'He gave me a lift from the airport. And he took me to Pompeii.'

'On a date?'

'As *friends*.' Lord. Anyone would think she was thirteen, not thirty!

Though they had ended up walking hand in hand at Pompeii. And had they not rescued the American tourist, Orlando might well have kissed her in the shadow of Vesuvius. Exactly the same way he'd kissed her in the surgery. And then…

Oh, she had to get a grip. 'I've been thinking about maybe retraining and doing family medicine. Orlando's a *medico di famiglia*, so he offered me a chance to work with him while I'm over here to see if family medicine suits me. And my boss said I can have a sabbatical. Which means I get the chance to spend the whole summer over here.'

'The whole summer?' Bartolomeo smiled. 'We would have more time together.'

'I'd like that,' she said.

'And this man, Orlando—he knows something about aplastic anaemia?'

'Probably as much as most family doctors,' Eleanor admitted. 'But the thing is, he worked in England for a couple of years. His English is perfect, so he'll know the medical terms in your language and mine—and he can help me talk to the consultant and find out what I need to know. But we'll need your permission to discuss your condition with your doctor.'

'Hmm,' Bartolomeo said, looking faintly suspicious. 'I don't know the man.'

'I do. And he's a good man. A good doctor.' Eleanor paused. 'Maybe we could have a drink together—a coffee, perhaps. And then you could decide, once you've met him.' She glanced at her watch. 'He might still be at his surgery, if he's not on a house call. I'll ring him now.'

Bartolomeo laughed. 'Something else you inherited from me. You're bossy.'

She smiled back. 'No, I'm efficient.'

His smile faded and he took her hand. 'Eleanor, I know I'm on borrowed time. I have you now, and I just want to enjoy you in the time I have left. It might be weeks, it might be months—and we might be very lucky and it will be longer.'

'And on the other hand we might not be lucky. I've just found you—and I'm not giving you up without a fight. I want time to get to know you.'

She lifted her chin fiercely. 'I have my mother's genes, too. So that makes me stubborn.'

'I can see that.' His eyes glittered with amusement.

'This isn't a condition I deal with in the emergency department. But I know where to start looking for the answers. I want to do some research on this and see what we can do. You're not in this on your own any more.' She squeezed his hand gently. 'You're with me. And together we're going to fight this.'

The glitter in his eyes was no longer amusement: she could see the tears forming.

'So will you meet Orlando? Talk to him?'

Bartolomeo dragged in a breath. 'All right.'

Still holding his hand with one of hers, she fumbled for her mobile phone, and flicked through the directory until she found the surgery number.

Chiara answered.

'*Buona sera*, Chiara. It's Eleanor. May I speak with Orlando?'

'*Un minuto*, Eleanor.' There was a pause. 'No, he has left for house calls. He has surgery later, at—ah, yes, four.'

'Can you ask him to call me, please? Tell him

it's about…about Bartolomeo.' Good as Chiara's English was, Eleanor doubted that she'd be able to translate the English condition to Italian either—and she didn't want to involve Alessandro or Giacomo.

'Of course. *A presto.*'

'*A presto,*' Eleanor echoed. '*Grazie*, Chiara.' She cut the connection and flicked through to Orlando's mobile number. The chances were his phone would be switched to divert or voice-mail—but if it was the latter she could at least leave him a message.

To her relief, it was voicemail. 'Orlando, it's Eleanor. Please can you ring me?' She left him her number.

Bartolomeo finished his coffee. 'Eleanor, *cara*, I hate to say it but…'

'You're tired,' she said gently. She could see that. 'You need some rest. I'll leave you in peace.'

He smiled ruefully. 'Once I could walk through Naples all day and dance all night.'

She squeezed his hand. 'I don't think I could do that, and I'm younger than you!'

'What will you do with yourself this afternoon?'

'Be a tourist,' she said. 'Visit churches and

museums and eat cake.' Actually, she had other plans, ones which involved finding an internet café so she could do some research. 'And maybe tomorrow you can eat *gelati* with me. Show me where they sell the best *gelati* in Naples and introduce me to your favourite flavours.'

Eleanor took the metro back to her hotel and asked for directions to the nearest internet café. Armed with coffee—which she ordered *molto caldo*, not caring that it marked her as a tourist because she really didn't like her coffee the lukewarm Italian way—a pen and paper and two hours' credit, she started her research, moving from journal to journal and paper to paper until she found what she was looking for.

She was halfway through when her mobile phone rang.

'Eleanor Forrest,' she answered crisply.

'It's Orlando. Chiara gave me your message. What's up?'

'I've found out what's wrong with Bartolomeo.'

'And it's serious?' His voice radiated concern.

'Aplastic anaemia.'

There was a pause. 'I don't know much about the condition, *tesoro*. I can look it up in my books for you, but you really need to talk to a specialist. A haematologist.'

'That's why I need your help.' She paused. 'I know you have surgery now, so could we meet this evening?' It was Friday so he'd probably be busy, but she crossed her fingers and said, 'After dinner? Say, nineish?'

'Fine. I'll meet you at your hotel, then we'll go to a bar or somewhere we can talk.'

'Thank you.'

Eleanor read through the last few papers online, then headed back to the hotel. It was still hard to take in: the fact that she'd found a family to belong to again, and was going to have it snatched away before she'd even had the chance to get to know Bartolomeo properly.

Even a quick chat with Tamsin didn't lift her spirits. Despite her best friend's teasing.

'So have you found a gorgeous man for your fling yet, then?'

Yes. 'No.'

'Ah, I get it—you're walking around with your eyes closed. Because we both know that Italian men are gorgeous, with a capital G.'

'Mmm.'

'Seriously, are you having a good time in Italy?'

'Yeah.'

There was a pause. 'What's wrong, hon? You said Bartolomeo was nice. Or were you just saying that to stop me worrying about you?'

'Bartolomeo's lovely. But...' Eleanor dragged in a breath, then told Tamsin what she'd discovered.

'Oh, no. That's *so* unfair.' Sympathy radiated through Tamsin's voice. 'Look, do you want me to come over?'

'They wouldn't allow you to fly, seeing as you're in the last trimester of pregnancy—and, no, I don't want you taking the risk and telling the airline staff you're just fat. I'll be fine. But thanks anyway.'

'You call me whenever you need to talk. Well, I know you know that, but it doesn't hurt to say so. And, Ellie, just for the record, Bruce and I think of you as family. That's why we asked you to be godmother to our baby. So you're not alone. You've got us.'

Eleanor had to blink away the tears. 'Tam, you're making me cry.'

'All right, so no airline will take me as a passenger. But flying isn't the only way to get to Italy. I can get the ferry across to France and drive—'

'No, Tam. Honestly, I'll be fine. But thanks for the support. I appreciate it.'

'And I've got a friend who works in Haematology—I'll give her a ring and see if she can give me some ideas. We'll talk tomorrow, OK?'

'Yeah. Thanks, Tam.'

'Any time. And I mean that.'

At precisely nine o'clock that evening, Orlando walked through the revolving doors into the hotel foyer. Eleanor was just walking down the stairs—his eyes were drawn to her straight away. Wearing a simple black dress and mid-height heels, and carrying the tiniest handbag, she looked stunning. And with her dark hair cut short, she reminded him of a 1950s film star. All she needed was a pair of elbow-length gloves, a chiffon stole and a set of matched pearls.

Dio, she was beautiful.

And was it his imagination, or were her dark eyes full of tears?

Her voice had sounded so flat on the phone.

Given that she'd recently lost her mother, the news of Bartolomeo's illness—and its likely prognosis—must be particularly hard for her to take.

He wanted to pull her into his arms, hold her close, comfort her—but here and now wasn't the place or the time. He held himself in check and simply joined her at the foot of the stairs. '*Buona sera*, Eleanor.'

She didn't return his smile. 'Good evening, Orlando.'

He didn't ask her what was wrong. He already knew. 'Let's go somewhere we can talk,' he said, and shepherded her out of the hotel to a small bar just down the street. It was crowded and noisy—but it was anonymous. Everyone was too busy to look at them or join in their conversation. Just what they needed.

'May I get you a drink?'

'Thanks.'

'What would you like?'

'Oh…' She spread her hands, as if thinking about what to drink was too much effort. He could understand that: she'd had a bombshell today, and her mind was probably churning round and round the issues. 'Anything,' she said finally, shaking her head as if she really didn't care.

He played it safe and bought her a glass of pinot grigio; he ordered a double espresso for himself. He had a feeling he was going to need the caffeine hit.

'*Grazie,*' she said when he returned to their table. She took a sip of wine, then turned the stem of the glass round and round between her fingers. 'I've only just found him. And now I'm going to lose him, Orlando. It's so bloody *unfair.*'

'Is he on the list for a bone-marrow donor?'

Her face tightened. 'You know as well as I do there aren't enough donors. It's hard enough to get people to give blood, let alone bone marrow—especially as giving bone marrow or stem cells is a hell of a lot more complicated than giving a pint of blood.' She dragged in a breath. 'I can't bear this. Just when I thought maybe I wasn't alone in the world after all, I have to…' She covered her face with her hands. 'I have to deal with it all over again. Losing the last person in the world who shares my blood.'

Seeing her pain made his own heart feel as if someone had taken it and wrung it out. And he couldn't stand by and just watch her crying. He scooped her onto his lap and wrapped his arms round her, holding her close to him. 'Ah, *mia bella.*'

He rested his cheek against her hair—lord, how soft it was and how sweet she smelled, like spring flowers—and stroked her back comfortingly. 'It will be all right, *piccolo.*' Though he knew he was lying to her. Without a transplant, the outlook for Bartolomeo was bleak. It was just a matter of time. But Orlando needed to reassure her, comfort her, make her feel better.

He shifted to kiss the top of her head. She burrowed closer. And suddenly his senses all went haywire.

Ah, hell. He shouldn't be so damned selfish. Her heart was breaking and all he could think of was how much he wanted her, how much his body was going up in flames, how much he wanted to carry her to her bed. What kind of man was he?

But then she shifted again so her cheek was against his. He could feel the dampness against his skin—what could he do but kiss her tears away? His mouth brushed against her cheek, moved lower, brushed against hers.

And then she was kissing him back. Just as she had when he'd kissed her for show in the staffroom. A proper kiss. Urgent and hot. The crowded bar just melted away as the kiss deepened. There was just the two of them...

Guilt kicked in sharply and he broke the kiss. 'I'm sorry, *tesoro*. I shouldn't be pressuring you like this. It isn't fair.' He should be protecting her, comforting her—not thinking about making love with her and losing himself inside her.

Her hands were shaking as she stroked his cheek. 'It wasn't just you. I was there, too.'

Again, the chatter in the bar faded to a distant hum. All he was aware of was Eleanor.

'Orlando...I don't want to be alone right now,' she told him. 'I'm so sick of being alone.'

Was she asking him to...? Ah, hell. He felt like the worst kind of bastard—right now he was taking advantage of her when she needed comfort. He needed to take a step back. Before it was too late. Before they both regretted it. 'Eleanor, listen to me. This is a bad idea. I can't promise you for ever. I don't believe in l—'

She put her finger over his lips, silencing him. 'I know,' she said huskily. 'And I understand.'

Did she? He wasn't so sure. She wanted a family to belong to—a family he couldn't give her.

'And I'm not asking for for ever.' She swallowed hard. 'I don't do this sort of thing. I don't…proposition men. But tonight…I need you tonight, Orlando. Stay with me tonight. Make me forget all this.'

His self-control was splintering rapidly by the second. 'This is a seriously bad idea,' he said, while he still had the strength to resist the appeal in her dark, dark eyes. 'You're upset, and I'm not going to take advantage of you. I'll see you back safely to the hotel.' A vision of their bodies tangled together between clean white sheets made his head spin. No, he didn't dare take her to the door of her room. He didn't trust himself enough. 'I'll escort you to the foyer.' He was speaking slowly, he knew—very slowly—but every word was an extreme effort: most of his energy was concentrated in trying not to kiss her. 'And I'll call you tomorrow morning.'

In answer, she leaned in and kissed him.

'Eleanor, God help me, I'm trying to do the honourable thing,' he told her when she broke the kiss. Every word, every breath was a struggle. His body was screaming out to carry her to her bed.

'What if I don't want you to be honourable?'

Oh, lord. He couldn't even try thinking of clinical chemistry and reference intervals to distract his body because his mind had simply stopped functioning.

She wanted him as much as he wanted her.

With a huge effort, he managed to say, 'So, as you said yesterday, all cats are grey in the dark?'

'No. I just want you.' She swallowed hard. 'I don't do this sort of thing. But I haven't been able to stop thinking about you since last week. Since you kissed me.'

'It was meant to be for show.'

'It didn't feel like it.'

'You kissed me back,' he pointed out.

She dragged in a breath. 'I don't even remember much of the rest of the day after that.'

'Neither do I,' he admitted. 'Eleanor, I don't think I have any blood left in my head. It's all gone south. But while I can still just about string a sentence together, let me tell you that I don't sleep around.'

'Neither do I.'

'So if we're going to...' Heaven help him, there was no 'if' about it. They were going to make love. Soon. Very soon.

Not soon enough, because every one of his nerve-endings was on fire.

'We need to get something?' she said.

'Yes.' With his last bit of self-control, he asked her, 'Are you sure about this?'

'Stop talking,' she said huskily, 'and kiss me.'

CHAPTER EIGHT

ELEANOR didn't remember going back to the hotel. She knew they must have called at a late-opening pharmacy or something on the way, because Orlando had mentioned the need for protection—but all she was aware of was his arms holding her close, the hard warmth of his body against hers, his clean masculine scent.

When the lift arrived, to her relief, they were the only ones waiting.

'Which floor?' Orlando asked, his voice husky with desire.

'Third.' She could barely force the word out. Couldn't think straight, she wanted him so badly.

He pressed the button; as the doors closed behind them, he rested his hands either side of her on the wall of the lift and bent his head to hers. The walls were mirrored, so she could see their reflections kissing, stretched out in an infinite line.

Right now she didn't want this to stop. Ever.

The lift glided to a halt and the doors opened again.

He broke the kiss and stared at her, looking dazed. His mouth was reddened and slightly swollen; she knew that hers would be in a similar state. That it would be obvious to anyone who saw them that they'd just been kissing each other stupid.

And she didn't care. She wanted him to kiss her again. And again. Until she forgot the whole world.

'Room...uh...number?'

Ha. He couldn't string a sentence together either, then.

As if he'd guessed her thoughts, he kissed her again, and her mind went blank. 'Number?' Ah. Key. It would be on the key. She fumbled with the zip on her tiny handbag and took the cardkey. 'Three-oh-five.'

To her shock, he scooped her up into his arms and carried her down the corridor; she was forced to slide her arms round his neck for balance. Eleanor was about to protest and ask him to put her down when he stopped outside her door. He brushed his mouth against hers, then let her slide all the way down his body until her feet touched the floor again.

She was aware that they were in a public place—that it was obvious to anyone who saw them exactly what was going to happen, the minute her door closed behind them—but the desire that flooded through her pushed everything else out of its way. And, judging from the hardness of Orlando's body, it was the same for him, too. Need. Urgency.

Key. Where was the cardkey? Oh, yeah. She was still holding it. She nearly dropped it, then it wouldn't fit into place and she almost growled with frustration. She didn't want to wait another second. She needed Orlando right now. Needed to feel his body inside her. Needed him to make her forget the world.

'Oh, why won't this bloody key work?' The words ripped from her in frustration.

'Relax, *piccolo*,' Orlando whispered against her ear, the warmth of his breath sending a shiver of pure lust down her spine. He took the cardkey from her and pushed it into the slot. And at last, at long last, the door swung open.

'*Dio*, I am glad your bed isn't a single,' he said

as he switched on the overhead light and pushed the door shut behind them. 'I need space for what I have in mind. And a light that's a little less harsh than this.'

The curtains were already closed; Orlando worked rapidly through the bank of switches next to the bed until the soft glow of the bedside light came on and the glare of the overhead light disappeared.

'Better. Much better,' he whispered, and pulled Eleanor back into his arms. His mouth dipped down to hers, taking tiny nibbles until she was practically whimpering, and then he deepened the kiss, exploring and teasing and inciting.

In the lift, she'd thought her desire was at a peak.

She'd thought wrong.

Orlando's mouth was stoking her desire higher and higher, and his hands were stroking the curve of her bottom, moulding her against him so she could feel the heat and hardness of his erection against her. It left her in no doubt that this thing between them was driving him just as crazy.

When he broke the kiss, he traced a path of kisses along the curve of her jaw. She tipped her head back, wanting more, and he nibbled his way down her throat to her collar-bones. She gasped as the tip of his tongue pressed against the pulse beating madly in her throat.

'Orlando. I need... Please...'

'Shh, *bella mia.*' Gently, he laid one finger over her lips. 'We have time. And I don't want to rush this.'

Unable to resist, she took the tip of his finger into her mouth and sucked it.

His eyes widened and he shuddered. '*Porca miseria!* Do you have any idea what you do to me, Eleanor?'

'The same as what you do to me,' she admitted. 'I hope.'

'Eleanor, I want this to be good for you, too. But you drive me so crazy, I don't think my self-control is going to last very long.' He stole another kiss. 'I want to touch you and taste you and look at you and fill my senses with you.'

Italian charm. She knew that was all it was. But, oh, it worked. More than worked. He blew her mind.

His English was still perfect, but voice was deeper now and his accent had become more Italian. She'd never heard anything so sexy.

Slowly, he unzipped her dress and eased it down over her shoulders to her waist.

'*Dio*, your curves,' he breathed, looking at her with his hands resting on her shoulders. 'So beautiful.' His hands skated over her shoulders, sliding her bra straps down her arms. 'You're amazing. Soft and sweet and the sexiest woman I've ever met.' His breathing was shallow and his hands were shaking as he touched her. His voice was a ragged whisper as he added, 'And I want you so badly, *tesoro*, it actually hurts.'

He traced the edge of the cups of her bra with one finger, making her shiver with need. This wasn't enough. She needed him to touch her much more intimately. Ease the ache. Tip her over the edge of fulfilment.

'I'm going to enjoy every second of this,' he told her. 'Every touch and every taste and every whisper of your voice. I want it to last a long, long time—yet at the same time I'm going to go crazy if you don't rip my clothes off right now and take me to your bed.'

Oh, so tempting. How she wanted to. She even placed her palms flat against his chest, ready to slide her fingers into the edges of his shirt and pull. But the feel of the soft silk shimmering against her skin made her stop. 'Your beautiful shirt. I can't treat it like that.' With shaking hands, she undid the buttons and slid it from his shoulders, the same way he'd pushed her dress down to her waist.

Lord, he was perfect. Broad shoulders, defined musculature, a light sprinkle of hair on his chest that arrowed down towards a very visible erection. Perfect. And all hers, for tonight.

She hung his shirt over the back of the chair; he followed her, slid his arms round her waist and pulled her back against him. His mouth grazed along the sensitive curve between her shoulder and her neck, making her shiver and lean back against him.

He dealt with the catch of her bra and let the garment fall to the floor. Her breasts spilled into his hands; she gasped as his thumb dragged across the tips of her nipples. The friction was good, but it wasn't enough. Not nearly enough.

'Orlando. Please. I need…' She couldn't get the words out. Could hardly breathe, she wanted him so much.

His mouth brushed the nape of her neck. 'Me, too, *tesoro*.'

She twisted round in his arms and kissed him, sliding her hands into his hair. The dark curls were fine, silky beneath her fingertips. Every inch of her skin felt sensitized, and even though his touch was light, it made her burn.

She wasn't sure who removed whose clothing, or when, or how. The next thing she knew they were both naked and he was carrying her to the bed. He pushed the cover to one side and laid her down on the cool smooth sheets, then knelt between her thighs.

'*Bella mia,*' he said softly. 'I ache for you.'

She ached for him, too. He was beautiful—built like an athlete, sturdy and muscular, no hint of fat. Just strong, ardent male.

'I want you so badly, Orlando de Luca,' she whispered. 'Make love with me. Please.'

'*Con piacere.*' His voice was actually shaking. 'With pleasure.' His fingers splayed over her stomach; his hands moved with feather-light touches, yet it didn't tickle. Her skin just felt hotter and hotter where he touched her. As if she were slowly being consumed by desire.

'You're so beautiful, Eleanor. All curves.' He skated around the edge of her breast with the tip of his index finger, and she tipped her head back against the pillow.

'More,' she murmured.

She reminded him of a medieval princess, lying back and commanding him to touch her. All she needed was the long hair spread over the pillow and a tiara. He couldn't help smiling.

'What?' she asked, frowning slightly.

'You remind me of a *principessa*—a princess. We really should have the four-poster and the velvet drapes.'

'Sir Orlando. I can imagine you coming home from the battlefield on your white charger.' She sat up and stroked his cheek. 'Was there a Sir Orlando?'

'In Italian literature, there's *Orlando Innamorato*—the tale of the knight Roland, who fell in love with the beautiful princess Angelica and tried to win her favours.' Just as he was winning Eleanor's. 'Though he went mad when she fell in love with another man., and was finally restored to sanity by a magician.' He turned his head slightly to the side so that he could kiss her palm. 'That story's called *Orlando Furioso*. "The Madness of Orlando." And right now I'm a little crazy, too, Eleanor. I need to touch you. Taste you.'

In answer, she brought her other hand up to his face, slid her fingers into his hair, and drew his mouth down to hers.

He couldn't remember the last time he'd wanted someone so much. Everything about Eleanor Forrest attracted him—body, mind and heart. Her skin was so soft, she smelled good, and the need he felt for her made him dizzy.

He broke the kiss, and gently lowered her back to the bed. Kissed the curve of her neck, the hollows of her collar-hones, and nuzzled his way down the valley between her breasts.

He teased one nipple with the tip of his tongue, until she arched on the bed and slid her fingers back into his hair. He smiled against her skin, then took her nipple into his mouth and sucked.

Her breathing had changed, he noticed, become needy little gasps. Good. He planned to make her forget everything except him. He kissed his way over her abdomen and slid one hand up her thigh. When she shivered, he cupped her sex with one hand.

'Yes. Oh, please.'

Hot and wet and so ready for him. He touched and teased and explored until she was shuddering, almost hyperventilating. Her eyes were tightly shut.

Was she thinking about Jeremy, the man who'd asked her to marry him when he'd already been committed elsewhere?

Well, he was going to drive that image right out of her head. Starting now.

'Open your eyes, *innamorata*,' he commanded softly. He wanted her to see him. So the next time she closed her eyes in pleasure, it would be his face she saw in her mind. 'Open your eyes.'

She did—and he saw the very second that her climax hit her. Saw the way her gaze became opaque. Heard her gasp his name. Saw the shudder of pleasure that rocked right through her.

So he'd been able to make her forget the world, forget her worries—forget everything except the fever pitch of desire between them.

Bene.

* * *

When Eleanor finally floated back to earth, she found herself lying in Orlando's arms. He'd tucked her protectively into his body; her head was resting on his shoulder and her arm was draped round his waist.

She could hardly believe he'd been so generous. He'd made sure that she was satisfied and had left himself frustrated. Given her time.

'Orlando. *Innamora*—' She stumbled over the word

He smiled and brushed a kiss against her mouth. '*Innamorato* is what you say to me.'

'Like the title of the poem,' she remembered aloud.

'Exactly like that. Except I think you're much more beautiful than the princess Angelica.' He stroked her face. 'And you're certainly not spoiled.'

Wasn't she? 'Orlando...I wasn't expecting that. That you'd...' She swallowed hard, trying to work out how to say it.

'Make sure you came first? *Tesoro*, I'm not quite that unselfish.' His laugh was wry. 'That's why I told you to open your eyes. So you'd see me and know that I was the one making you feel that way.'

She shivered. 'I wasn't thinking of Jeremy.'

'Good. But just in case you were…' Gently, he manoeuvred her onto her back and slid his hand between her thighs again.

She was shocked to discover how quickly he could arouse her again. When he kissed her, she matched him hunger for hunger, bite for bite, stroke for stroke.

Exploring his body was a revelation. Jeremy had always seemed faintly embarrassed about sex. Orlando clearly enjoyed it, encouraged her to touch him and even showed her exactly how he liked being touched. And because he was so bold about it, Eleanor wasn't in the least self-conscious: she even found herself enjoying it, discovering how to make his breathing become faster and shallower and how to make him arch in pleasure, his fists curling round the head-board.

He murmured something in Italian—something she couldn't quite catch.

'Orlando?'

His eyes snapped open and he stared at her. 'What?'

Tension radiated from him. Did he think she'd changed her mind and was going to tell him to stop? 'You spoke in Italian,' she explained. 'I'm sorry, I couldn't follow.'

Immediately, his tension dissolved, and he smiled. *'Mi dispiace, tesoro.* Oh, hell. Here I go again. I'm sorry. I, um, forgot to think in English.'

'What did you say? I mean, I understood that last bit. It's the bit before where you lost me.'

A slow smile spread across his face. 'Ah. That.'

'Orlando?'

'It might shock you.' He kissed her, a sweet kiss that turned into a slow burn of pleasure. 'What I said was, "I need to be inside you, Eleanor,"' he said huskily.

She nibbled at his lower lip. 'Guess what? I need you inside me.'

He slid his hand between her thighs. 'Now?'

'Right here, right now,' she confirmed.

He moved to unwrap a condom and roll it on. Then he frowned. 'You're smiling. What?'

'Just thinking.'

'Tell me.'

'You don't actually keep a stock of condoms on you.'

His frown deepened. 'No, I already told you I don't. That's why I had to buy some.'

'So you don't take, um, every opportunity that comes your way.' And with a man as gorgeous as Orlando, there would be opportunities. Plenty of opportunities.

'I told you before, I'm picky.'

'Mmm, and you're beautiful.'

This time, he laughed. 'You can't tell a man he's beautiful.'

'Oh, yes, I can. Look at you. Like one of the gorgeous statues you see in the museums and art galleries here. Perfect.'

Her fingertips trailed across his skin, down his chest to his abdomen, and he groaned. 'Don't tease me, Eleanor. I can't wait any more.'

'Neither,' she said, 'can I.'

And she stopped thinking as his body eased into hers.

CHAPTER NINE

THE next morning, Orlando woke to find himself wrapped around Eleanor, with a sheet half covering them and half on the floor. The rest of the bedclothes were probably also on the floor; and he realised with a flicker of guilt that she was balanced virtually on the edge of the bed. He had the lion's share of the pillows, too.

Last night had been...amazing. He knew he should've left last night—or at least in the early hours of the morning. But she'd asked him to stay with her. Hold her until she slept. And, heaven help him, he hadn't been able to tear himself away. Even worse, he hadn't *wanted* to stay away—if she hadn't asked him to stay, he would've suggested it.

And they'd woken twice in the night, feasted on each other.

They'd gone through a whole packet of condoms.

Oh, this was *bad*.

He'd told Eleanor he didn't do relationships. That he didn't believe in 'The One' or love or happy ever after.

She'd said it didn't matter.

But had she, with that weird female logic, decided that maybe she could change his mind? Would she expect him to stick around this morning? Would she think that what they'd shared last night meant he'd decided that maybe love did exist?

What really scared Orlando was that he was beginning to wonder it himself.

Oh, lord. He needed a cold shower to shock some common sense back into his head.

From where he was curled around Eleanor, he could see the clock on the bedside table. Nearly seven o'clock. It was his turn to run the practice's Saturday morning surgery this week. He could hardly turn up dressed in what he'd worn last night—besides, his doctor's bag was at home. He needed to leave. Now.

Eleanor seemed to be sleeping soundly. If he

was careful, he'd be able to untangle himself from her, get dressed, write her a note and leave her sleeping. Avoid all that horrible morning-after awkwardness. And then maybe they could meet for dinner. Back on the old footing. And everything would be just fine.

He was just starting to move away from her, very gently, when Eleanor rolled onto her back and opened her eyes.

'Good morning, Orlando.' She gave him a soft, trusting smile that made him feel like a real louse. Oh, lord. How could he possibly leave now?

And, for his own peace of mind, how could he possibly stay?

Orlando definitely had a rabbit-in-headlights look on his face, Eleanor thought. Frozen in panic and desperate to run.

'I...' He swallowed hard. 'Good morning, Eleanor.'

It was clear to her that he regretted what had happened last night. Though she hadn't exactly given him a chance to refuse, had she? She'd cried all over him in the bar and asked him to stay with her because she was tired of being alone. She'd actually begged him to make her forget the world.

He had.

What they'd shared last night had been amazing. And she was sure that it had been mutual. But this morning the real world had come back to smack them both in the face. Orlando had made it clear he didn't do relation-ships—and nothing had changed.

'I...um, I'm on duty this morning,' Orlando muttered. 'At the surgery.'

Oh, for goodness' sake. Did he really have to make such an obvious excuse? Embarrassment flooded through her, making her temples throb.

'Listen...about last night,' Orlando said.

Oh, no. That was one of the most cringe-making phrases in the English language. The one that made people apologise and shuffle their feet and offer excuses. It made her want to bury her face in the pillow and howl. Instead, she strove for coolness. Never again after Jeremy would she let a man know he'd hurt her. And weren't the English meant to be good at this stiff-upper-lip business? 'Don't worry about it.' She yanked the sheet up to cover herself. 'We both know where we stand.'

He rubbed a hand over his face. 'Eleanor, I—'

Don't let him say he was sorry. She couldn't bear hearing that. 'I know. You need to go home and change. I'll, um, catch you later. And don't worry, I won't look while you're getting dressed.'

Disappointment made her voice catch. She'd thought there was something between them. That Orlando felt the same pull of attraction she did. Or maybe he was one of those men who just liked the thrill of the chase without the manacles of commitment. Hadn't the fiasco with Jeremy already proved beyond reasonable doubt that her judgement in men was lousy?

'Eleanor, I really do have to work. It's not an excuse. It's my turn to do the Saturday morning surgery and I need to collect my doctor's bag from home first. And I need to change into the sort of clothes our patients expect me to wear.'

She didn't dare meet his gaze.

'I'm not expecting you to shadow me today. Not on a Saturday.'

That definitely sounded as if he wanted some distance between them.

'Maybe we could, I don't know, have a late lunch somewhere overlooking the sea?'

Eleanor had a nasty feeling that this was his way of softening what he wanted to say. Over lunch, he'd give her the 'Dear Jane' speech about how it wasn't her, it was his fault and he was a louse, yada yada yada.

Well, she didn't want to hear it.

If he thought it was a mistake and it shouldn't have happened, then she wanted to be the one to say it first. She still had *some* pride left. 'You really don't need to do that. I'm a big girl and I can take responsibility for my own actions.' She took a deep breath. 'We both know last night shouldn't have happened. I was upset and I took advantage of your good nature.'

'*Cara*, *I* am the one who took advantage of *you*.'

'No, you didn't.' She still couldn't bring herself to meet his eyes. 'I'm the one who asked you to stay. And I'm not under any illusion that you're going to declare undying love for me. You were honest with me from the start. You told me you don't believe in love.'

There was a long, long pause. 'So where does it leave us now?' he asked.

'As we were. Fr—' She changed her mind in mid-sentence. 'Acquaintances.'

'And colleagues?'

It'd be hard to explain to Serafina, Alessandro, Chiara and Giacomo why she'd suddenly vanished from the practice. Though, at the same time, how could she work with him now?

Complicated.

Or maybe it'd be easier if they did work together: a working relationship would slot a nice neat barrier between them, precluding a more personal relationship.

'The offer to work in our practice is still open,' he said. 'You were planning to stay in Italy for a while. And I'm not intending to break my promise to help you with the paperwork and to find a place to live.'

'I'll sort something out myself.' She took a deep breath. 'But there is something I need your help with.'

'Of course,' he said immediately.

Relieved that she'd let him off the hook so easily? It stung, so she couldn't help saying, 'Careful, you don't know what I'm going to ask you.'

'Ask me, then.'

This time, she did look at him. 'Will you come to Bartolomeo's house this afternoon? Talk to us—as a doctor—about the aplastic anaemia.'

He frowned slightly. 'His doctor might not be too happy about that.'

'I'll deal with that when I have to. Will you help me?'

He nodded.

'What time can you make it?'

'Three?' he suggested.

'Perfect. I'll see you then.' She found a piece of paper and scribbled Bartolomeo's address on it. 'Have a good morning at the surgery.'

He opened his mouth as if to say something, then closed it again. She turned away as he slid out of the bed and feigned interest in a guidebook about Naples while he dressed.

'I'll see you later, then,' he said at the doorway.

'*A presto.*' She didn't look up from her book until she heard the door click behind him. Then she sat up in bed, drew her knees up to her chin and wrapped her arms round her legs. What a mess. She didn't regret last night—how could she, when she'd discovered so much pleasure in his arms?—but she really, *really* regretted this morning. She regretted the awkwardness between them. And most of all she regretted the knowledge that she'd been stupid enough to hope for something more than Orlando was prepared to offer her.

At five to three, Eleanor answered the door to Orlando. 'Come in,' she said. She ushered him through to the terrace where Bartolomeo was sitting and introduced them quickly. 'I'll fetch coffee,' she said.

It had finished brewing—just—when she walked into the kitchen. And when she returned to the terrace with the tray of coffee she could virtually see the tension between Bartolomeo and Orlando. They were speaking so rapidly that she couldn't follow what they were saying, but she could tell by the tone that things were getting a little heated.

'Perhaps one of you could be courteous enough to translate for me?' she asked, pouring them both a cup of coffee.

They exchanged a glance, and then Bartolomeo said ruefully, 'Orlando was telling me that if you could understand what I was saying, you'd go bananas because you're an independent woman who's perfectly capable of making her own decisions and doesn't need her father to grill a man about his intentions towards her.'

Bartolomeo was playing the heavy father?

And Orlando was doing the angry-young-man thing?

She looked at them both in disbelief, and then burst out laughing. 'Oh, honestly! The pair of you!'

'I'm glad you can see the funny side,' Orlando said dryly. 'But your father accepts now that we are colleagues and this is a professional matter.'

Which pretty much summed up their relationship. That morning she'd called him an acquaintance. He'd referred to her just now as a colleague. Last night had been...an aberration. Something they wouldn't repeat.

'Eleanor's qualified medically but she needs my help as a translator—someone who understands both languages and medical terminology. So may we have your permission to talk to your consultant about your condition?' Orlando asked.

Bartolomeo looked at both of them, and sighed. '*Si*. All right.'

'That's settled. Good.' Eleanor folded her arms

and looked at Orlando. 'We could sit here and be polite. But I think it's better if I say it straight.'

For a second, alarm flitted over his face. Did he really think she was going to bring up last night? She didn't want Bartolomeo knowing just how naïve and foolish she'd been. 'We need to talk about a bone-marrow transplant. My bone marrow will be compatible with my father's.'

Orlando sucked in a breath. 'You're saying you want to donate bone marrow?'

Bartolomeo's hand shook as he replaced his coffee-cup in the saucer, making the china clatter. 'Eleanor, *piccolina,* you can't do this.'

'Yes, I can,' she said. 'We already know the supportive therapy isn't going to cure you. It's helping—but clearly it's not helping enough, because you're still tired. My best friend Tamsin is a GP—a *medico di famiglia,* like Orlando— and she has a friend who works in haematology.' For Bartolomeo's benefit she added, 'Disorders of the blood, like thalassaemia and aplastic anaemia. They talked last night and Tamsin called me this morning. She says that definitive therapy—in other words, a bone-marrow trans-plant—will restore healthy, working bone marrow. And then you won't need the blood transfusions any more.'

Orlando held up a hand in protest. 'Hang on—you're rushing things. There's Bartolomeo's age to consider, and transplants are usually done from a brother or sister or a matched unrelated donor.'

Eleanor's mouth tightened. 'Bartolomeo's sisters are not a match. He has no brothers. And you know as well as I do, the risks of rejection are much lower in an allogenic transplant from a blood relative than they are in a transplant from an unrelated donor. Which means me.'

Bartolomeo frowned. 'I'm not happy about this. What about the risks to you?'

'They're low,' Eleanor reassured him. 'I'm thirty years old, I'm perfectly healthy, and I'll recover quickly.'

'How quickly?' Bartolomeo asked.

'That depends on how the marrow is harvested,' she admitted. She didn't want to lie to him. But she didn't want him worrying either. 'You know how a transplant works?'

He wrinkled his nose. 'Vaguely.'

Which meant he didn't. Probably nobody had explained it to him because nobody had thought it was an option. Until now. 'There are three parts to your blood—red blood cells that carry oxygen round your body, white cells that fight infection, and platelets that help stop you bleeding. The blood is made with stem cells in your bone marrow—that's the spongy stuff in the middle of your bones. If your bone marrow isn't working properly, your body can't produce blood. So right now you need a transplant of bone marrow to help your body make the blood cells.'

'How it would work,' Orlando chipped in, 'is that we test the donor's blood to see if the tissue type matches yours. If it does, then we would give the donor a full medical examination and counselling.'

Eleanor rolled her eyes. 'There's no "if" about it. I'm Bartolomeo's daughter. You can even see the family resemblance, for goodness' sake! As his daughter, I've inherited three out of my six antigens from him. So our tissue types will match.'

'You would still have to undergo counselling,' Orlando said.

'I don't *need* counselling over this.' Didn't he realise? Wasn't he listening? 'Bartolomeo is my father.' Her only living blood relative. Who was dying. And it was in her power to save him. 'I want to do this. And, yes, of course I need to undergo a medical examination, but I can tell you now the results will be fine.'

'You need counselling,' Orlando repeated stubbornly.

'Then help me fast-track it. Because I'm not going to change my mind,' Eleanor informed him coolly.

Orlando glared at her, then turned to Bartolomeo. 'For a week or so before the bone marrow is taken from the donor, we give him or her injections of growth factor to produce lots of stem cells in the bone marrow.'

'So it hurts?' Bartolomeo asked.

'No,' Eleanor reassured him. 'The injections are done in the arm or the leg.' And sometimes in the abdomen, but she thought it politic not to mention that. She grinned. 'Hey, I'm a doctor and I work in the emergency department, so I see needles all the time. I'm not scared of needles.'

'I loathe needles,' Bartolomeo muttered. 'So then they take out the bone marrow? How? Does it hurt?'

'The donor has a general anaesthetic,' Orlando said. 'The operation lasts for an hour, maybe two, and the surgeon collects the marrow cells from the pelvis with a needle and syringe.'

'There's no cutting or stitching involved, and I'd be able to leave hospital the next day,' Eleanor said. 'Then the bone marrow would be given to you in the same kind of way as you have a blood transfusion—there's a thin plastic tube called a Hickman line that the surgeon would put in your neck or your groin, and the healthy marrow travels through your body and settles in the spaces in the middle of your large bones. Then hopefully in the next fortnight to a month your body will accept the new bone marrow and start producing new healthy blood cells.'

Bartolomeo looked impressed. 'I thought you said you were an emergency doctor? I didn't think you did that sort of operation in the emergency department.'

'I am, and we don't,' Eleanor said. 'But I've been researching the procedures since you told me about the aplastic anaemia, and my best friend's haematology colleague filled in the gaps for me.' She smiled at him. 'It's pretty straightforward. Though before the operation you'll need radiotherapy or chemotherapy to destroy your remaining bone marrow cells, so there's less risk of your body rejecting the donated cells.'

Orlando frowned. 'That's not suitable for all patients, Eleanor. And it might be too stressful for Bartolomeo's body.'

Given his age, she knew that was true. 'There are other ways,' Eleanor countered. 'Such as a non-myeloablative stem cell transplant, with smaller doses of drugs and chemo to lower his immune system enough to accept the donor cells.'

Bartolomeo waved both hands. 'Hello, I am still here! Don't talk over me—I'm not following half of what you're saying now. Non-mye—what?'

'Non-myeloablative,' Eleanor said. 'Sorry. I didn't mean to talk over you. Or talk jargon.' She'd just wanted Orlando to realise that she knew exactly what she was getting into. She needed him on her side. Needed him to help her convince the consultant to give her father the life-saving treatment he so desperately required. 'Non-myeloablative just means treatment that won't destroy your bone marrow. Normally if a cell goes into your body that your body doesn't recognise as its own, your immune system will kick in to destroy the invader—so if we don't lower your immune system before the transplant, you'll be at risk from something called "graft versus host disease".' She smiled at him. 'If we lower your immune system, it won't attack the bone marrow cells from my system when we transplant them to your body. For a while, our cells will be mixed, and eventually mine will replace yours.'

'After the transplant, you'll need medication to stimulate the production of blood cells, and you'll have blood tests to check the new bone marrow is working,' Orlando said.

'More needles,' Bartolomeo said wryly.

'Though I should warn you that while you recover, you're likely to pick up infections because your immune system will be so low,' Eleanor continued. 'You need to avoid anyone coming near you who has a cold.'

'We can try to minimise it by giving you antibiotics, so the infections don't get a chance to take hold,' Orlando said. 'But as well as the medication, you'll still need blood transfusions to maintain the right level of blood cells in your body until the new bone marrow is working. It's demanding, Bartolomeo—very demanding, physically and emotionally. And it can take a long time to recover.'

'How long?' Bartolomeo asked.

Orlando took a deep breath. 'I have to be honest with you. It could take as much as a year.'

Eleanor glanced at her father. A year's recovery was a much better prospect than having no time at all, in her eyes. Did he feel the same? Oh, please. He had to. She couldn't bear the idea of losing him so soon after she'd found him. 'Often it's less than that,' she said.

'And you, Eleanor?' Bartolomeo asked. 'What side effects will it have on you?'

'Hardly anything,' Eleanor said swiftly.

Bartolomeo scoffed. 'Orlando, you took the Hippocratic oath, yes? So tell me the truth. Tell me what Eleanor is trying not to tell me.'

She tried kicking Orlando's ankle under the table, but he ignored her. 'A donor might have bruising and soreness in the lower back and in the place where the bone marrow was taken. It'll last for a few weeks. And while the bone marrow renews itself the donor will feel tired and should avoid strenuous exertion. It may take a week or so to recover.'

'That's if we go for a traditional bone-marrow harvest under a general anaesthetic,' Eleanor argued. 'There's a newer procedure called PBSC, which stands for peripheral blood stem cell donation. What that means is that I'd have daily injections of a growth factor to increase the number of stem cells and make them move out of my bone marrow and into my general circulation. Then the surgeons simply hook me up to a special machine that separates out the stem calls from the rest of my blood cells. The procedure's called leukapheresis. Basically the blood goes out of one arm, gets filtered, and goes back into the other arm. The doctors collect the cells in two separate sessions, each lasting about four or five hours, so I won't need to stay in hospital overnight. I won't need any anaesthetic either—definitely not a general and not even a spinal block, so you can take out a huge chunk of risks there.'

Bartolomeo folded his arms. 'And the side effects?'

Eleanor smiled. 'I might feel a bit fluey, but a

donor can go back to their normal job within twenty-four hours of a PBSC.'

'The success rate is good?' Bartolomeo asked.

'Between forty per cent and seventy per cent,' Orlando said.

'And it's getting better,' Eleanor added.

Bartolomeo looked thoughtful. 'So how new is this process?'

'It's becoming more and more common,' Eleanor said. 'And it's much better for the donor and the person receiving the stem cells. On the donor's side, it's not an invasive procedure, doesn't involve a general anaesthetic and has a shorter recovery period. On your side, it means you'll spend a shorter time in hospital, and your white blood and platelet counts return to normal more quickly so there's less of a chance of complications.'

'It still doesn't mean you can definitely do it,' Orlando warned. 'You inherited one set of haplotypes from Bartolomeo and one from your mother—if your mother's haplotypes are a bad mismatch for Bartolomeo's...'

Eleanor's jaw set. 'Only one way to find out. I want that blood test. First thing tomorrow morning.'

Orlando shook his head. 'Tomorrow's Sunday. You're not going to get a test on Sunday.'

'Then we'll do it Monday. I'll pay for a private test if it's quicker.'

Bartolomeo put his hand over hers and squeezed it. 'I can't ask you to do this for me.'

'You're not asking,' Eleanor pointed out. 'I'm offering. We've been through this, Bartolomeo. You're my only blood family, I've just found you, and I'm not prepared to stand by and lose you before I get the chance to know you properly. If donating a few of my stem cells will keep you around a bit longer, I want to do it. And do it *now*.'

Bartolomeo stared helplessly at her. 'I don't know how to thank you.'

'You don't have to. You're my family.'

CHAPTER TEN

THEY managed small talk for another half an hour, then Eleanor, noticing how tired her father looked, called a halt. 'You need a rest,' she said gently. 'I'll leave you.'

'I'll see you back to the hotel,' Orlando said.

'No, it's fine. I'm sure you have things to do.'

'I said,' he repeated, 'I'll see you back safely to the hotel.'

It was fairly obvious he wanted to talk to her about something—something he didn't want to say in front of Bartolomeo. Well, if he wanted a fight, he'd get it. She was still furious with him for spelling out the bleakest side of the bone-marrow donation and worrying her father. *'Grazie,'* she said quietly, hugged Bartolomeo goodbye and followed Orlando outside.

As soon as they were seated on the metro,

Orlando shot her a sidelong look. 'You really sprang that one on me.'

She folded her arms. 'Don't be ridiculous. I told you I needed your help talking to my father's consultant about the aplastic anaemia. And that I'd been researching it.'

'But you didn't warn me you were going to offer to be a donor.'

She rolled her eyes. 'Oh, come off it. Isn't it the obvious solution?'

Orlando mirrored her stance, arms folded. 'May I point out that you only met the man a few days ago? And you're proposing to undergo a very painful operation for someone you barely know.'

She glared at him in outrage. 'How can you say that? He's my *father*!'

'You told me yourself you didn't even know he existed until a couple of weeks ago.'

She shook her head in disbelief. 'I know you've got a problem with families, Orlando, but don't dump your insecurities on me.'

He gave a mirthless laugh. 'I don't have any insecurities.'

'No?' They'd shared the ultimate closeness the previous night, and the way he'd walked out on her so easily this morning still rankled. 'The way I see it, Orlando, you can't understand why anyone might want to show some commitment to another human being, because you can't do it yourself.'

He rolled his eyes. 'Don't tell me you think this is about last night.'

'Isn't it?'

'No,' Orlando snapped. 'This is about *you*. About the fact you're rushing in to something without thinking it through properly. You said yourself, a bone marrow donation is complicated—that's why it's hard to get donors. It isn't an easy option, Eleanor. It's not like giving blood.'

She lifted her chin. 'A PBSC is. Virtually.'

'It's more complicated than that, and you know it. It takes a lot longer, your blood is filtered, you have to take drugs beforehand, and you can't just get up and carry on as normal after a cup of tea and a biscuit. And you're proposing to do this,' he repeated, 'for someone you barely know.'

He really, really didn't get this, did he? She frowned. 'If I were donating blood marrow to someone on the transplant list, it'd be to someone I didn't know. What's the difference?'

'The difference is you're vulnerable right now

and you're setting yourself up for heartbreak because there's no guarantee it's going to work. If you were an unrelated donor, there wouldn't be the emotional involvement: you'd be sad if it didn't work, yes, but it wouldn't really affect you. In this case, if it doesn't work, you'll be devastated. You're pinning all your hopes on something that isn't one hundred per cent guaranteed—on something that basically has a fifty-fifty chance of working, if you look at it objectively.' He raked a hand through his hair. 'And before you bring it up, I'm not proud of the way I took advantage of you last night. I've already apologised for that.'

He didn't say it, but she could see the question in his eyes. *What else do you want from me?*

He'd told her the truth, right from the start. He didn't do commitment, didn't believe in love. What was the point in asking him for something he couldn't give?

She swallowed the lump in her throat. 'I'm sorry. I'm just...'

'I know.' He reached out and stroked her cheek. 'I'm sorry, too. But you need to think about what you're doing here, Eleanor. Don't rush in blindly.'

She knew he was right, and it made the comment sting even more. And the gentleness of his touch... It hurt. Because she knew he couldn't give her more, and she was ashamed of herself for wanting more. She pulled away from him. 'So what am I supposed to do? Bartolomeo is my only living blood relative. Am I supposed to just stand by and watch him die slowly?'

'No, of course not.'

'His sisters aren't a match, there isn't a matched unrelated donor available, and the chances are that my bone marrow will be a match for his. Yes, you're right in that I haven't known him long. But I want time to *get* to know him. The only way I'll get that time is if he has a bone-marrow donation. From me. What other way is there?'

He was silent, and her rage died as quickly as it had blown up. 'I'm sorry. I'm upset about the situation and I shouldn't take it out on you. But you need to understand where I'm coming from, Orlando.'

'I do.'

'Really?' She didn't think so. 'I'm completely alone in the world. I have good friends, and I'm grateful for that, but it's not the same as having someone to belong to. It's not the same as being part of a family.'

'And that's what you want?'

'Doesn't everyone? Don't you?'

He shrugged. 'I don't need that. I'm happy as I am.'

'Are you? I mean, *really*? Don't you look at your friends—at Serafina and Alessandro, at your friends in London with your godson—and wonder what that special something is they have?'

'No.'

She stared at him. 'You're unbelievable. Are you seriously telling me you think they're going to split up?'

'No. Just that confetti doesn't last for ever. Honeymoons end. After that, you just have to make the best of it.'

'You're horribly cynical.'

'I'm a realist, *tesoro*.'

'So last night...'

He flinched. 'How many times are you going to make me apologise for that, Eleanor?'

She shook her head. 'That's not what I was going to say. Last night there was a connection between us.' She felt the colour seep into her face. 'Apart from the physical, I mean. Are you telling me it wasn't the same for you?'

There was a long, long, pause. 'I don't know,' he admitted finally.

'Then why did you agree to help me?'

'Because I'm a nice guy?' he suggested.

She shook her head. 'You could've pleaded pressure of work. Or maybe put me in contact with a specialist you know. But you haven't. You came with me to meet Bartolomeo yourself. You're giving me support.'

'As I would any colleague.'

She reached over to run her thumb over his lower lip. 'If you were the kind of man you're trying to make me believe you are, this wouldn't affect you. But your pupils just dilated.'

'That's merely a physical reaction.'

She shook her head. 'There's more to it than that, and you know it. It isn't just sexual attraction. When you kissed me at the surgery. When you held my hand at Pompeii. Every time you're near me. I know how it makes me feel—and I think it's the same for you. Or are you going to lie to me as well as to yourself?'

He didn't answer, and as they reached her stop, she stood up. 'I'll see myself back.'

'I said I'd see you back, and I keep my word. Look, I'm trying to be completely honest with you,' Orlando said, following her off the train.

'Honest?' she scoffed.

'Yes. I like you, Eleanor. A lot. And I find you attractive. The way I feel about you...' He swallowed hard. 'All right. You want honesty? I've never felt like this about anyone before. If you must know, it scares the hell out of me because I've no idea what I'm doing. Though what I do know is that I'm making a complete mess of things,' he added wryly.

'What do *you* want, Orlando?'

He shook his head. 'How can I answer that? I don't believe in love. I've seen my mother like this, so sure her current love was The One—the man she wanted to spend the rest of her life with. And then I watched the disillusionment set in when she realised he wasn't, and saw a good relationship sour into contempt and hatred. Time and time again. She's been divorced five times, and in and out of love more often than I can count. I don't want that to happen to me. To *us*.'

He took a deep breath. 'Look, I know you want to be part of a family. I can tell you now mine's a mess. Stepsiblings and ex-stepfathers I don't see, a father I can barely remember from my childhood. I don't know if I can give you what you want out of life.'

'Then it's simple,' she said as they reached hotel. 'Don't bother.'

Orlando watched her disappear through the revolving doors, feeling as guilty as hell. What was wrong with him that he couldn't just tell her that he wanted to take the chance—to see if their relationship could grow and develop into something really special? Tell her that he was beginning to believe in 'The One'—and that she was it, for him?

'You,' he informed himself as he walked home, 'need your head examined.'

No. What he really needed to do was apologise. Ask her if they could start again.

It was just a question of working out how.

Eleanor spent a restless night, not sure whether she was more furious with Orlando for being difficult or with herself for having such lousy judgement in men.

She'd just dragged herself out of the shower the next morning when there was a knock at the door.

Huh? She hadn't ordered room service.

Pulling her dressing-gown tighter, she opened the door a crack.

'Dottoressa Forrest? I have a delivery for you.'

It was the most beautiful hand-tied bouquet of roses and freesias. She frowned. 'Are you sure it's for me?'

In answer, the maid handed her an envelope addressed to Dottoressa Forrest.

'Thank you,' she said, accepting the flowers with a smile and then fumbling for her purse so she could tip the maid. 'Um, where would I be able to buy a vase?'

'I can bring one for you,' the maid said with a smile. 'I'll get it now.'

'*Grazie.*' Eleanor set the arrangement on the dressing-table and opened the envelope. There was a small card inside.

I apologise. We need to talk. Please meet me for breakfast. I will be waiting for you in the foyer. Orlando.

Right at that moment she wasn't sure she

wanted to see him. But she got dressed anyway. When the maid had brought the vase, Eleanor arranged the flowers. So Orlando wanted to see her. And he was waiting downstairs in the foyer. Did this mean he'd brought the flowers himself? Come to think of it, florists didn't usually deliver on a Sunday.

So he must have been waiting for at least ten minutes.

Good.

He could wait a bit longer.

She managed to hang it out for another fifteen minutes before she went downstairs. Immaculately made up, so he wouldn't be able to see the shadows under her eyes and guess that she'd slept badly. She was going to play this so cool she'd be the queen of the Antarctic.

He was sitting in one of the chairs, ostensibly absorbed in a newspaper. But she could tell that he had one eye on the stairs, because the moment she started walking down them he folded the newspaper and stood up.

'*Buon giorno*, Eleanor.'

'Good morning, Orlando.' She wasn't in the mood to compromise. Even though he had sent her flowers. 'Thank you for the flowers,' she added politely.

'They were the least I could do.'

'I didn't think florists were open on Sunday mornings.'

'The Mercarto dei Fiori—the flower market—by the Castel Nuovo is open at sunrise every morning.'

'So you picked these yourself?'

A slight smile curved his mouth. 'Yes, but I admit that the stall-holder arranged them for me. Hand-tying a bouquet is a little beyond my skills.' His smile faded. 'I owe you an apology. I'm sorry, Eleanor.'

She inclined her head in acknowledgement.

'Will you join me for *la prima colazione*—for breakfast?'

His eyes were huge; he looked as guilty as a puppy who'd been caught chewing a favourite pair of shoes. And when he gave her a smile that beautiful… Even though she was still angry with him, how could she say no? 'All right.'

'*Bene.* Would you prefer to stay here, or go to a little place I know round the corner that does the best almost croissants in Naples?'

She'd bought pastries to go with morning coffee

at the practice a couple of times the previous week, so he knew her weakness for them. Particularly almond croissants. She made the effort to sound cool, calm and collected. 'As you wish.'

'Then let's go.'

When they were ensconced in the little *caffè*, with a *lattè* each and a plate of almond croissants between them, he looked at her.

'You look as bad as I feel.'

She stared at him for a moment, not quite be-lieving what she'd just heard. Was this his idea of a truce? 'Oh, thank you.'

He noticed the acid edge to her tone and winced. 'That came out wrong.' He raked a hand through his hair. 'I used to be good with people. No, I *am* good with people. With patients. It's just…you.'

She'd noticed. But she also knew he wasn't going to say the words. And, without those, she definitely wasn't playing.

'Let me start again. I feel horrible about the way I behaved towards you yesterday.' He took a deep breath. 'I'm not offering any excuses. I don't do relationships—well, only the very lightest ones—and the fact I'd even consider something different with you scares me stupid.'

She opened her mouth to speak, and he lifted a hand to forestall her. 'No, Eleanor, please, hear me out. I've been thinking about what you're doing, and even though I don't agree with you completely I can understand why you want to do it. But you can't do it on your own—even though your Italian's come on in leaps and bounds, you might feel groggy in the hospital and not be able to follow what people are saying or make them understand what you want. You need someone with you. A support person. So I'm proposing…'

Her heart did a funny sort of wiggle and she dug her nails into her palms. He didn't mean *that* sort of proposal, and she knew it.

'I'm proposing that I'm that person. Your support person,' he emphasised.

When she said nothing, he continued, 'I made some phone calls this morning. Certain people owe me favours. So I called them in. I've arranged tissue typing. I'll take the blood from you myself, first thing tomorrow morning—any future procedure will be done by the doctor at the hospital, but if we wait to register you with another doctor the paperwork will take for ever. Time I know you don't want to waste.' He paused. 'And it's your decision whether you spend your mornings at the practice or not this week. No pressure.'

She could only focus on the first bit. He'd arranged tissue typing. He was going to support her, help her as much as he could with the bone-marrow donation. 'You'll do the blood test,' she echoed.

'And I'll take the blood over to the hospital in my lunch-break. It takes five days to get the results, so if I'm there by about half past one we'll have the results on Saturday afternoon. In the meantime, I'll register you with the practice, so Alessandro or Giacomo can be your doctor—not me, because it's not ethical.'

'They're my colleagues, too,' she pointed out. 'So are you saying things are different between us—that you don't see me just as a colleague?'

A muscle tightened in his jaw. 'Don't interrupt.'

'You can't run from this for ever.'

'I'm trying to focus on practical things, Eleanor.'

'Do you or do you not see me as just a colleague.'

'What do you want, blood?' He gritted his teeth. 'All right. I admit I don't see you just as a colleague. But don't give me a hard time over this, because right now I'm not in the mood for dealing with it,' he told her. 'Now, as I was saying, we can arrange a full medical examination—with your permission—to save time when we get the results back.'

'If I'm a match.'

'If. But, as you say, Bartolomeo is your father. Unless your mother's haplotypes clash badly with his, the odds are that you will be a match.' He looked at her. 'This is going to be a big deal, Eleanor. Physically and emotionally. You're not going to have room in your life for...other stuff.'

Other stuff. He meant the attraction between them. The way they hadn't been able to keep their hands off each other on Friday night. The way he'd kissed her in the surgery. The way their hands had kept touching, the way they'd kept looking at each other and wondering. 'That's a cop-out.'

He smiled wryly. 'Maybe.'

'Come on. You know it is.'

'It is also, perhaps, buying time.'

She frowned. 'How do you mean?'

'My head's all over the place right now. But I do know one thing I definitely don't want.'

She was almost afraid to ask. 'What's that?'

'For you to walk out of my life. That's a first for me. I've never felt that about anyone before.'

'And you want to take things slowly.'

'Until I'm sure,' he said. 'Look, you've been badly hurt. It's going to take time for you to trust again. And I never trusted in the first place. It's going to take time for me to learn.'

'Time. Which Bartolomeo doesn't have,' she said.

'Exactly. If the transplant goes ahead, the procedure will take days, weeks. Time when we have space to think, to sort things out in our heads—well, *my* head,' he admitted, 'but we're not apart either.'

'That sounds suspiciously like having your cake and eating it.'

'I'm not that arrogant.' He spread his hands. 'I don't want to hurt you, Eleanor. If we rush this, it's going to go wrong. Badly. We both need time to get to know each other better, be sure what we both want. This will give us that time.'

He was being sensible, she knew. Though it hurt that they'd shared the ultimate closeness and he still wasn't sure how he felt about her.

'Eleanor?'

She considered it. What other option did she have? Finally, she nodded. 'All right. The other stuff goes on hold. Until Bartolomeo's had the transplant and we know whether it was successful.'

'And I'll support you through this.' He held her gaze. 'As your friend.'

CHAPTER ELEVEN

ON MONDAY morning, twenty minutes before Orlando's first patient was due in, Eleanor sat on the chair next to his desk with her arm propped on a pillow, exposing her inner elbow.

'Before we do this, I need to know something because it might affect the results,' Orlando said. 'Have you had a blood transfusion recently?'

'No. For the record, I've never had a transfusion.'

'That's good. Now, make a fist for me.'

He used his thumb to probe for the vein in her inner elbow; although the gesture was completely impersonal and professional, one she'd done herself countless times, the touch of his skin against hers still made her heart beat faster.

Stop being so pathetic, she told herself silently.

'I thought you said you weren't scared of needles?'

'I'm not.'

He gave her a half-smile. 'That's not what your veins are saying. They've gone into hiding. Squeeze and release your fist. And again. And again.' His smile broadened. '*Bene.* You'll feel a sharp scratch.' And then he was fitting a test tube to the end of the syringe, and deep red liquid was trickling into it.

Eleanor was silent while he took the blood sample, then switched to a second test tube and then a third. She tried to crack a joke. 'How much do you want, a whole armful?'

He regarded her seriously. 'You're having a full medical as well as tissue typing. We're looking at Us and Es, full blood count, glucose—the usual blood work-ups. We need to check your renal function and your liver and your thyroid.'

'There's nothing wrong with my kidneys or my liver or my thyroid.'

He ignored her. 'And we need to be sure you haven't picked up anything that might compromise Bartolomeo's system.'

'I was teasing about the armful.'

He gave her a half-shrug, finished taking the sample, then placed a pad of cotton wool over the injection site before removing the needle. 'Press on that. It'll mean you're less likely to bruise.'

She already knew that, but assumed it was his way of trying to put some professional distance between them—treating her as if she were a patient. And talking about procedures was safe. It meant she'd concentrate on work instead of emotions—it'd help her ignore the way her skin tingled when he touched her, even as impersonally as taking a blood sample. 'So what happens now?'

'For the tissue typing, the haematologist will look at about ten different DNA markers. The important ones are the recognition ones—the antigens that tell the immune system whether to attack or leave them.'

'So they'll be looking at chromosome six,' Eleanor said. 'The MHC—the major histocompatibility complex. And there are a large number of proteins involved, so it's rare to find a perfect match with the human leucocyte antigens.'

'It doesn't need to be a perfect match,' Orlando reminded her. 'Just good enough. Remember Bartolomeo has had several blood transfusions, so he'll already have a large number of antibodies circulating against HLAs. When they test the

HLAs, if your A, B and DR ones match, we'll be fine.' He paused. 'Your blood groups need to be compatible, too. If your blood group is O, it's the universal group so you can help anyone.'

Eleanor knew what he'd left unsaid: if her blood group clashed with Bartolomeo's, it wouldn't work. Her blood group wasn't a rare type, though: it was the second most common. 'I already know my blood group. It's A,' she said. She dragged in a breath. 'Don't say we're going to fall at the first hurdle. I know that my blood group means that his has to be A or AB for this to work.'

Orlando picked up his phone and handed it to her. 'Call him. Find out. And if it's A…'

'Check if he's positive or negative. I know.'

Two minutes later, she had the answer. 'A-positive. Same as mine.'

'*Bene.* Had you been O, it would still have worked. Except he would have acquired your blood group because your bone marrow will be making his blood cells in the future.'

'You've done a lot of research on this, haven't you?'

'I checked a few extra things yesterday,' he

admitted. 'Like you, I was able to get access to a haematologist.'

'And he was helpful?' The question was out before she could stop herself.

Orlando clearly knew exactly what she was asking. 'Yes, *she* was,' he said coolly. 'And, just for the record, she's old enough to be my mother.'

Eleanor flushed. 'I…' Oh, lord. Talk about putting her foot in her mouth. And what gave her the right to be jealous anyway? They weren't officially an item.

'This is what happens when you put emotions into things. It gets messy,' Orlando said dryly. He labelled the test tubes and took them to the practice nurse's room to store it in the samples fridge. 'I'll take this over myself at lunchtime,' he said. 'And you are going to have to be patient for the next five days. I've already pulled strings so the test results will be available on Saturday—we would normally have to wait until Monday.'

'Thank you.'

'It's not just the HLA we're looking at—I'm asking for other blood tests as well. You work in emergency medicine.' He looked grim. 'I should have asked you this before. Have you ever had a needlestick injury?'

'No.'

'Good. Any scares of any sort?'

'I'm not with you.'

'Maybe there was an emergency—maybe a case like the one on the plane, where you didn't have the right equipment with you but you were morally bound to help. Say you rushed in to help someone, didn't have gloves on, they were bleeding and maybe there was a cut on your hand—and obviously you wouldn't know if your patient was HIV-positive when you treated them. So have you been exposed to blood that might have been infected?'

'No.'

'Good. So, Eleanor.' He leaned back against his chair. 'Are you spending your mornings here this week?'

'I've been thinking about that all weekend,' she admitted. 'Working with you is going to be a strain.'

'Unless you keep your emotions out of it and treat me as you would any other colleague.'

She wasn't sure she could do that. And he'd

admitted that he didn't see her as just a colleague, either. 'If I have to wait for five whole
days with nothing to do except wonder what the
results of the tissue-typing and medical tests will
be, I'll go crazy. I need to keep busy.'

'Then the decision is easy. Work with me. Our
first patient is due in about…' he glanced at his
watch '…five minutes. Do you need a plaster
for your arm?'

She stopped pressing on the cotton wool and
removed it. No telltale oozing of blood. 'No,
I'm fine.'

'And no bruise.'

Which was a good thing. Because she might
not have been able to stop herself asking him to
kiss it better.

When their first patient came in, Orlando introduced Eleanor. 'Signora Giordano, this is
Dottoressa Forrest—she is an English doctor,
working with me for the summer. Would you
mind if she sat in on our consultation?'

Signora Giordano smiled shyly. 'No.'

'She might ask questions, but I will translate
for you,' Orlando reassured her. 'Would you step
on the scales for me?'

Signora Giordano sighed. 'I've been trying to lose weight, really I have. I walk the dog twice a day.' She took the pedometer from the waistband of her skirt. 'Ten thousand steps a day. And still the weight won't come off.'

'I know you're trying hard,' he reassured her.

Eleanor read the display on the scales and tapped the figures into Orlando's computer. 'No change since last month,' she said quietly.

Orlando translated rapidly, then took Signora Giordano's blood pressure. 'Still a bit on the high side,' he said. 'If it's like this next month, we'll need to change your drugs. How are you feeling in yourself?'

'A bit low,' she admitted. 'My family say I've lost my sense of humour. And sometimes I cry— but I just need to pull myself together.'

Low mood, struggling with her weight— Eleanor had heard this before. Tamsin's mother had had a similar problem. And, like Signora Giordano, she'd worn a cardigan even though it had been quite warm outside. And her eyes seemed slightly protuberant, too.

'May I look at the back of your hand?' she asked. At Signora Giordano's nod, she examined the woman's skin. 'It seems very dry. Do you need to use more hand cream than usual?'

'*Si*. And it doesn't really work any more.'

'And your periods, your *flusso mestruale*— how are they?'

Signora Giordano made a face. 'I haven't wanted to bother Dottore de Luca with it because it's not really an illness, but I have to get up a couple of times at night to…' She flapped an embarrassed hand. 'To change.'

Orlando exchanged a glance with Eleanor, as if he knew exactly where her questioning was going. 'And your energy, Signora Giordano?'

'I get tired,' she admitted. 'I go to bed earlier than I used to. But that's my age.' She put a hand to her mouth. 'I'm too young for the menopause, surely!'

Eleanor glanced at the screen to check Signora Giordano's date of birth. Forty-two. 'Unless your mother and sisters went through the change very early, yes, you're a little young for that. *Permesso*, it's a very personal question, but making love with your husband is, um, less than it used to be?'

Signora Giordano blushed. 'We work hard. We're too tired.'

The symptoms were really adding up. 'I'm sorry, these questions must be embarrassing for you, but is there any change in your toilet habits?'

'It's more difficult to go, yes—the pharmacist said I needed to drink more and do more exercise.'

'That's better than using laxatives, yes,' Eleanor agreed, 'but if it's not working you need to talk to us about it. I would like Dottore de Luca to give you a blood test, because I think you may have an underactive thyroid.'

'Your thyroid is a gland in your throat, just below your voicebox,' Orlando explained. He reached over to touch Eleanor's throat in demonstration, and her skin felt hot where he touched her. 'It regulates your energy—as Dottoressa Forrest says, we need to do a blood test to check, but I agree with her that your thyroid is probably underactive. Your symptoms all add up to a clinical picture.'

'But they're all such silly things. I didn't want to waste your time,' Signora Giordano protested.

'Singly, they're little things, but together they add up,' Eleanor said gently. 'Heavy periods, constipation, tiredness, dry skin, lower libido and slight depression. I think your thyroid isn't working as it should, and the earlier we spot it the earlier we can do something to make you feel better. We can treat it with tablets—we'll have to increase the dose gradually until we get the right one, or you'll feel really ill.'

Orlando swiftly took a blood sample. 'Come back and see us next week when the results are back,' he said. 'And then we can talk about your treatment.' He smiled at her. 'And I can promise you, you'll soon start to feel a lot better.'

'*Grazie*, Dottore de Luca—Dottoressa Forrest,' Signora Giordano said.

'*Prego,*' they said in unison.

'Good call,' Orlando said when their patient had left. 'You're a natural with family medicine. Have you come across this before?'

'My best friend's mum had it. I remember her symptoms,' Eleanor said. 'And you picked up on what I was thinking.'

'We work well together,' he said. 'A good team.'

Yes. But was that going to be enough? Eleanor wondered.

On Wednesday afternoon, Orlando went with Eleanor to see Bartolomeo.

'We won't know whether the tissue is a match until at least Monday,' Orlando warned. He'd agreed with Eleanor that they'd tell Bartolomeo the later date, so he wouldn't be uptight, waiting for the results, if they were late.

'But there's a chance. Hope,' the older man said, his eyes glittering.

'Well, I'm staying here in Italy for a while, regardless of what the tests show,' Eleanor said. 'So I'm going to look for a place to rent.'

'I have a spare room—more than one. And you're my daughter. You can stay here with me,' Bartolomeo said.

She stroked his hand. 'That's a lovely offer—but I'm used to having my own space,' she said quietly. 'So thank you, but no.'

'There are hardly any places to rent around this part of Naples,' Bartolomeo said, 'and I won't have you staying in a rough part of the city.'

'I won't move to a rough part,' she promised. 'Orlando will help me find somewhere—he'll tell me which areas I should avoid.'

The older man's eyes narrowed as he looked at Orlando. 'You won't let her move somewhere bad?'

'Of course not.'

'I'd still be happier if you moved in with me, Eleanor,' Bartolomeo said, his mouth compressed.

There was a solution. One that was going to test Orlando's self-control to the limit. One that was really a very bad idea indeed, given that he wanted to take things slowly. But the words came out anyway. 'I, too, have a spare room.'

Eleanor's eyes widened. 'You're suggesting that I move in with *you*?'

'That way, you're not far from your father but you have your independence. And if this transplant goes ahead, I'd rather you were staying with someone, not in an apartment on your own,' he said. 'I would recommend having someone to keep an eye on you for a few days.'

Bartolomeo's eyes widened. 'So there are risks with this procedure after all? Eleanor might be ill afterwards?'

'No, there aren't.' She glared at Orlando. 'He's scaremongering.'

'Actually,' Orlando said, trying to keep his tone as reasonable as possible, 'anyone who knows you, Eleanor, also knows you're likely to overdo things instead of resting the first couple of days. That's why I think someone should keep an eye on you. And who better than a fellow doctor?'

He'd told her he wanted time to think about things. Space between them. And what was he doing? Making sure she spent even more time around him. He must be crazy.

She clearly thought so, too, because she brought it up when he took her back to her hotel. 'I can't possibly move in with you.'

'Yes, you can. Look, do it for Bartolomeo's sake. He's worrying about you. And that means he's stressed. He already has enough stress lined up for when the transplant goes through.' Oh, lord. She had him at it now. Saying 'when' instead of 'if'. 'Think about it. It's the sensible option. And you, Eleanor Forrest, are a sensible woman.'

'Why does that sound like a insult?'

'Because your imagination is playing tricks on you. Look, it will stop your father worrying.'

'So I just move into your house.'

'To my spare room. You will have your own key, so you will be completely independent. Come and go as you please.'

'Won't I get in your way? Disturb you?'

She'd disturb him all right. Though not in the way she meant. 'No,' he fibbed. 'And when I am not on house calls, my car is at your disposal.'

'That's too generous. I'm perfectly capable of using public transport.'

She waved a dismissive hand—the sheer Italian-ness of the gesture amused him, but he didn't want her to get the wrong idea so he propped his elbow on the table and rested his chin on his hand, making sure to cover his face so she couldn't see him smiling.

'I have a weekly ticket,' she continued, 'so I can catch the metro, a bus, a tram, a funicular railway. No problem.'

'True. And I live reasonably near a metro station. But the offer is there. You might want to take Bartolomeo for a drive along the coast or something.'

She was silent for a while. 'If I move in—and I mean *if*—then I insist on paying you rent.'

He smiled. 'That's not necessary. I said I would support you through this.'

'Emotionally. You don't need to do it finan-cially. I'm, um—look, my parents left me a house and money. I don't need support in that way. And I would still expect to do my share. You know, chores in the house.'

He made a dismissive gesture. 'No need. I have a cleaner.'

'Cooking, then.'

'We'll negotiate that later.' He paused. 'So. Do I have a house guest?'

'Yes. *Grazie.*'

'OK. Do you want to check out now or tomorrow morning?'

She gaped. 'That's a bit fast!'

'It's Wednesday. If we get the results back on Saturday afternoon and if they're the right ones, you'll be starting treatment on Monday. Whatever we've said to your father, we don't know how you're going to feel. So it makes sense to move now, have a couple of days to settle in, just in case you start to feel rough.'

He was pushing her. He knew it. And he also knew it was crazy. If anything, he should be thinking up reasons why she *shouldn't* move in. Reasons to keep his distance.

But he yearned for her to be near.

And this was a way of doing it without having

to explain how he felt or probe the emotions he normally kept at bay.

'I need time to pack my things,' she said.

'Pack them. I'll go back to the surgery for a couple of hours and do some admin work, then I'll fetch the car and pick you up.' He glanced at his watch. 'I'll see you at five. *A presto.*'

CHAPTER TWELVE

AT FIVE o'clock exactly, Eleanor opened the door to Orlando's knock. 'Nearly done,' she said. 'I've finished packing. I just need to settle the bill.'

'Bene. I'll load your things into the car, then.' He smiled at her. 'Hold out your hand.'

She frowned, but did as he asked. He dropped two keys onto it. 'It's obvious which is which,' he told her. 'One is for the car and one is for the front door.'

'Thank you.' She took her keychain from her handbag and added Orlando's keys to it. It felt oddly intimate, having his keys nestle against hers. He trusted her with his keys. Would he trust her with his heart?

As soon as she'd settled the bill, she joined Orlando in the car and he drove them to his apartment. 'I live on the fifth floor,' he said, taking her baggage from the car and gesturing to the enormous ancient building in front of them. 'There is a lift.'

'This place is amazing,' she said as they travelled up. 'It's a *palazzo*, yes?'

'Yes. It dates from the fifteenth century, though it was converted into flats years ago, and my apartment was renovated not long before I bought it. One of these days I'm going to research it, find out who lived here.' He shrugged. 'I like it. It's convenient for work and convenient for the city.'

Smack in the middle of the city; she'd noticed plenty of shops and *caffès* on their way here. And yet the area wasn't that noisy: the palazzo overlooked a large pedestrianised square.

'Welcome to *mia casa*—my home,' he said softly, and opened the front door. 'I'll show you around.' He set her cases down in the hallway. 'This is the kitchen.' It was very modern, with stainless-steel appliances, maple cabinets with long tubular brushed aluminium handles, granite worktops and a dark slate floor, but it was definitely a kitchen for use rather than a kitchen for show. Pans hung from a rail, and there were fresh herbs growing in pots on the window-sill.

'Living room, dining room.' There was an arch between the two rooms; the walls were painted a bright sunny yellow, and the curtains at the large windows were white voile. Again, it was very modern—a glass-topped dining table with white leather chairs, with a state-of-the-art plasma TV and beige leather sofas in the living room. On the walls were framed prints of Whistler nocturnes.

But there was nothing personal there, she noticed. No photographs of family, no children's drawings made especially for a favourite uncle, not even any friends' wedding photographs. Nothing to give away who Orlando was.

And it was very much a single person's home—a young, single, urban professional person's home, she thought. Underlining the fact that Orlando wasn't a family man. Just like his consulting room in the medical practice, the room was incredibly neat: everything in its place. This wasn't an apartment that would echo with the laughter of children and have crayoned pictures stuck onto the fridge with magnets. There wouldn't be toys and books and socks scattered everywhere. Orlando was good with children—she'd seen him at work—but it was clear to her that he liked to keep them at a professional distance.

'My study.' It was painted a paler yellow, with a large desk, a state-of-the-art computer and tightly crammed bookshelves covering one wall. 'If you want to read anything, feel free to help yourself. I'm afraid I don't have many books in English, but you're welcome to use my library card—they have a reasonable foreign section.'

'Thank you.' She smiled wryly. 'It feels odd, thinking of English as a foreign language.'

'It is, here,' he pointed out. 'Feel free to use my computer, too—you don't need to find an internet café to research anything or check your email.'

'*Grazie.*' And she really was grateful for that: it meant she could have better contact with Tamsin, as well as researching extra information about Bartolomeo's condition.

'If you need to call anyone in England—your boss, your friends—you know the dialling codes from here.' He gestured to the phone. 'As they say in Italy, *mia casa è sua casa.*'

Tears pricked her eyelids. 'I really appreciate

this,' she said, hoping her voice didn't sound as cracked to him as it did to her.

He continued with the tour, dismissing the next door with a wave. 'My room and bathroom.' He led her to the door opposite. 'And your room and bathroom.'

It was gorgeous, Eleanor thought. White walls with the faintest hint of peach, white voile curtains and a wrought-iron bedstead with white covers. Like that in the rest of the apartment, the flooring was beech—the real thing, not laminate. The bathroom walls were a rich turquoise, teamed with a black and white diamond-tiled floor and a white suite.

Orlando either liked things very simple, or had found an interior designer whose tastes he could live with.

And how.

'Wow,' she said, feeling her eyes widen in pleasure.

But he'd left the best to last. A terrace with wrought-iron balustrading overlooking the piazza, with views of Vesuvius and the Bay of Naples. 'This,' she said softly, 'is incredible.' The perfect spot to linger with a mug of coffee or a glass of freshly squeezed orange juice. There were olive trees growing in terracotta pots in the corners of the terrace, terracotta troughs with a jumble of red and white geraniums between them, and a granite-topped bistro table with two wrought-iron chairs.

'Would you like to eat out here tonight?' he asked.

She blinked. 'Eat?'

'Uh-huh. I was planning to cook for us. If that's OK with you. Why don't you unpack while I sort something out?'

'Um, shouldn't I be helping you in the kitchen?'

'No need.' He smiled at her. 'And it's not a chore. I enjoy cooking. It helps me relax.'

Which meant he'd be good at it. Orlando, she thought, was good at everything he did.

Including making love.

Which she'd promised herself she wouldn't think about.

By the time she'd finished unpacking, the aromas emanating from the kitchen were making her seriously hungry. She followed her nose.

He looked up and smiled at her. '*Bene.* You've finished.' He handed her a glass of wine. 'Go and sit on the terrace. Take a book, if you want. I'll bring the antipasti through when it's ready.'

'Thanks.' She walked into his office. As he'd said, he had few English books. Though the bookshelves were clearly in some sort of order—medical textbooks, novels, poetry. Including *Orlando Furioso.*

Oh, lord. Her grip tightened on the stem of the wineglass as she remembered that night. *Orlando Innamorato.*

Except he wasn't, was he? He'd offered her a place to stay. As a friend, not as his lover.

In the end, she went onto the terrace and just sat gazing out at the view. She was so lost in thought that she didn't hear Orlando join her, and jumped when he spoke to her.

'What are you thinking of, Eleanor?'

She shook her head. 'Nothing important.'

'Worrying about your father? We are doing what we can. What will be will be.'

'Just don't break into the Doris Day version,' she said wryly.

He laughed and hummed, '*Que sera, sera*'. 'Have some food, Eleanor. Everything always seems better when you're not hungry.'

She felt her eyes widen as he placed the food in front of her. 'This looks gorgeous—and complicated.'

He spread his hands. 'It takes *ages*. Possibly—oh-h-h—ninety seconds' preparation.'

'You're kidding.'

'The hardest part is cutting the prosciutto into strips. Wrap it around the asparagus, add a thin slice of *dolcelatte*, put it in the oven for ten minutes, and that's it.' He shrugged. 'The simplest things are often the best.'

'It's gorgeous,' she said after the first mouthful.

He'd made an equally simple second course: grilled chicken and salad. Followed by a bowl of fresh strawberries and a pot of melted white chocolate for dipping. And then the ubiquitous espresso.

'Don't tell me. It's half-cold,' she said before he'd even poured it out.

'No. I know you prefer your coffee the English way.'

'Whereas Italians like the buzz of caffeine.'

He laughed. 'That's why you never see an Italian sitting in a *caffè*. Waste of time.' He spread his hands. 'Pay for your coffee, get your receipt, have it made for you, and down it on your way out. It's the way here in Napoli.'

'I noticed. And if you order a *lattè* or a *macchiato* after breakfast-time, they look at you as if you have two heads. It's easier to go to a tourist coffee-shop.'

'And pay four times as much for the privilege.'

Easy banter. But there was nothing easy between them; Eleanor knew that they were both aware of the undercurrent. Both avoiding the real issues.

And that night she lay awake in the wide double bed, knowing that he was sleeping just the other side of the wall. How easy it would be to walk into his room, climb into his bed and just ask him to hold her.

And how bad an idea that would be, too. He needed time—time to get used to the idea that maybe they had a future. That he wouldn't be like his mother, searching fruitlessly for The One and leaving a trail of broken hearts behind him. That she wouldn't be like his mother either and walk out on him when he failed to live up to whatever impossible ideal she had in her head. He'd let her this far into his life. She just needed to be patient.

* * *

Eleanor was surprised at how easily she'd settled in to life at Orlando's apartment. And on Friday afternoon, when Bartolomeo was too tired for company, she did a little shopping in the tiny delicatessens and speciality shops nearby, tried her hand bartering in the market, and finally pottered around the apartment before giving in to the impulse to call Tamsin.

'Right. Now you're talking to me, you can spill the beans. All of them,' Tamsin demanded. 'You are on your own right now, aren't you?'

'Yes. There's nothing to it. Orlando's just being a good friend.'

Tamsin groaned. 'I told you to have a fling with a gorgeous man, not go and live with him!'

'I'm not living with him. I'm staying in his guest room,' Eleanor corrected her.

'You're eating together and you're spending time in the evenings together—that counts as living together in my book. And you've already admitted he's drop-dead gorgeous.'

'We're just *friends*.'

'Yeah, right,' Tamsin said dryly. 'Just make sure you wait until I've had this baby before you announce you're staying in Italy with him. And I'm telling you now, if I'm not chief bridesmaid and wedding planner, you're in major trouble.'

'Number one, you're married and pregnant, so you'd be matron of honour,' Eleanor said.

'Stop splitting hairs.'

'And, number two, we're not getting married.'

'Living in sin, then. But you don't move over there permanently until I've had a chance to inspect him and made sure he's good enough for you,' Tamsin said darkly.

'Tam, it's not like that.'

'Hmm. We'll see.'

'So you really don't have to worry. Everything's fine,' Eleanor said, hoping that she sounded rather more convincing than she felt. She distracted Tamsin with talk about babies, but when she finally replaced the receiver her edginess returned.

Tomorrow was results day.

Please, please, let them be the right ones.

And if she didn't keep herself busy, she'd go crazy. She took the recipe she'd downloaded from the Internet and headed for Orlando's kitchen.

* * *

Orlando could smell the aroma of tomatoes and fresh herbs all the way down the corridor. He'd planned to take Eleanor out to dinner that night, to distract her from the fact that the results were due tomorrow, but clearly she'd been feeling antsy and taken matters into her own hands.

He closed the front door behind him, then walked quietly to the kitchen. He leaned against the doorjamb for a moment, just watching Eleanor as she chopped and stirred and tasted. Lord, she was beautiful. The way she moved… It was all he could do to stop himself striding over to her, yanking her into his arms and kissing her senseless. He just about managed to keep himself in check, then he said softly, '*Buona sera*, Eleanor. Something smells good.'

She looked over at him and smiled. 'Hi. I hope you don't mind me taking over your kitchen.'

'No.'

'I thought you might…' She bit her lip. 'Well, you don't like sharing your space.'

'I admit, it's strange,' he said. 'Coming home after surgery to a flat that isn't completely silent and empty—knowing the door's unlocked and you'll be curled up on the sofa with a book or listening to music. Domesticated.'

She looked faintly worried. 'And you hate that.'

The words slipped out before he could stop them. 'It's different with you.'

'How do you mean?'

'I... Nothing.' He made a dismissive gesture. 'Just ignore me.'

'Bit difficult when you're standing three feet away from me,' she pointed out. 'So how's it different with me?'

She wasn't going to let him get away with this one, was she? He sucked in a breath. 'OK. I admit, I like you being around.'

'And?'

Could she read his mind, or was it that obvious? 'And it scares me stupid at the same time,' he admitted. 'Because when this is all over, it's going to be messy. We're both going to get hurt.'

'You're assuming it will be over.'

She was calling him on this? He lifted his chin. 'My experience of families tells me that, yes, it'll end.'

'Not necessarily. My experience of families is different: it tells me that things *can* work out.

My parents were together for well over twenty years. And if they'd both lived they'd still be together now.'

'That,' Orlando said, leaning back against the wall, 'is what scares me. How can I live up to that? How can I give you what they gave each other when I don't know how it's done—when I haven't had an example to show me the way?'

She took the pan off the heat and walked over to him. Took his hand and raised it to her lips. Brushed her mouth, oh, so lightly over his palm. It made his whole body feel as if it had turned to flame. She curled his fingers over the place where she'd kissed him. 'Why don't you try trusting yourself? See where this takes us?'

Because he'd already seen what happened when people did that. Seen the tears and the wreck of the relationship. Too many times. 'I don't want to see you hurt when I let you down.' Just as his mother's husbands had never lived up to her expectations.

She frowned. 'You're here now, when I need you. What's going to change?'

'I can't answer that. I just know that one day we'll both wake up and everything will seem different. And I don't want to hurt you, Eleanor. The longer this goes on, the more it's going to hurt—me, as well as you.'

'This is all your decision. Don't I get a say in it?'

'No.'

'Why not?' she asked, her voice very soft.

'Because right now you've got a lot on your mind. You're vulnerable and you're not thinking straight.'

'And you are?'

Probably not. He found it very difficult to think straight when she was around. But he wasn't going to admit *that*.

At his silence, she dropped his hand and took one step backwards. 'So do you want me to leave?'

'Of course not. I'm not going to throw you out at a time like this. You're waiting for the test results. If all goes well, you'll probably be on treatment next week. And...' He raked a hand through his hair. 'I said I'd support you through this. I'm not the kind of man who goes back on my word.' He dragged in a breath. 'And that's why I can't promise you a relationship and say that it will last for ever and ever. I can't make a promise that I don't know if I can keep. Eleanor,

I can offer you my friendship and my support. And that's all.'

'I'd better get on with dinner, then.' She walked over to the hob again and continued with the sauce she'd been making when he'd come home.

He was about to protest that he didn't want to hurt her—but he knew he already had. Her British stiff upper lip was firmly in place. Brisk, no-nonsense. 'Eleanor. I'm sorry. I wish I could be different. I like you—I like you a lot—and I admit there's a physical attraction between us. But until I can promise you undying love, it's not fair to either of us to act on that. Let's get through the transplant. And then we'll have time to concentrate on us.'

'Sure.'

She didn't sound sure at all. She sounded utterly miserable—rejected, unwanted, unloved.

Lonely.

Ah, hell.

He couldn't leave it like this. He joined her at the stove, took the pan off the heat again and pulled her into his arms. Held her close, rested his cheek against her hair, breathed in her sweet scent. 'I'm trying to get my head around this. I swear, I'm trying.' And, lord, he was trying to be the man she needed him to be. He so wanted to be that man.

But could he?

Would he be enough for her?

'I just need more time, *tesoro*.' He let himself hold her for a few seconds longer. 'I just,' he whispered, 'need time.'

With a huge effort he let her go again. She was rigid, as if trying to hold her own emotions in check.

Domestic. Routine. That was what he needed right now. Something everyday that he could focus on, help him put his emotions back behind the fence where he normally kept them. 'How long is dinner going to be?'

'Soon.' She was clearly in the same state as he was, the way she was stirring that sauce when both of them could see it didn't need stirring.

'Shall I open some wine?'

'I'll do it. I meant to surprise you. Make dinner the same way you did for me.' She went to the fridge, took out a bottle of wine and poured him a glass. 'Go and sit on the terrace.'

His fingers touched hers as she handed him the

glass and it felt like an electric shock. He knew he was being a coward, but he was glad to escape to the terrace and stare out at Vesuvius. Hell, the way she made him feel, his emotions were like the volcano in mid-eruption. Turbulent. Hot. Overwhelming.

Why couldn't he let himself believe? In her—in himself—in love?

The breathing space did them both good, because when she reappeared on the terrace, carrying a platter, he was able to smile calmly at her, and she no longer looked near to tears.

'I cheated with the antipasti,' she said. 'There was this gorgeous little deli round the corner.'

She'd brought out a plate with an arrangement of his favourites. Black olives, chargrilled artichokes, sun-dried tomatoes and grilled sweet peppers. She'd included tiny cornets of cured ham, anchovies and slices of *scamorza*.

'It's perfect,' he said.

The main course was even better. 'An authentic Napoletana sauce, too,' he noted. 'I'm impressed.'

'It's not hard to follow a recipe.'

'Even so.' He raised his glass to her. 'It's lovely. *Grazie.*'

Although his head was telling him he really needed to get some distance between them—that he should make some excuse to skulk in his office for the rest of the evening—his heart reminded him that she needed the company. Needed the distraction. Tomorrow could make or break her.

There was one thing that would distract both of them…

But no. The timing was wrong. He wasn't that much of a louse, to put his needs first. So he sat with her. Talked to her. Taught her a few Italian phrases, introduced her to some of his favourite music. Just about managed to stop himself kissing her goodnight.

Though he slept badly. And from the shadows under her eyes at breakfast the next morning, so had she.

As the minutes dragged by, the tension in her body racked up until he could almost see waves of it flowing out from her.

'Come on. We'll go to the hospital. The long way round,' he said, 'because waiting there for the results will be even worse. We'll play tourist on the way, have an early lunch out.'

'Mmm-hmm.'

She was too tense even to be polite, he noticed. Well, he wouldn't take it personally. What she really needed, he thought, was a hug. But he didn't trust himself to stop at a friendly hug. A walk and negotiating the public transport system would help him get his impulses back under control again.

Although he pointed out particularly interesting architecture and told her little snippets about the bits of Naples they passed through, she didn't seem to take anything in. She barely touched lunch. And by the time they reached the hospital, the strain was really showing on her face: she'd lost all colour on her face and her expression was pinched. Haunted.

Right now she needed him. He slid his arm round her shoulders as they made their way to the consultant's office. Maybe she'd find comfort in the warmth of his body; maybe she'd find strength in his strength.

'Dottoressa Forrest? Gilberto Marino. A pleasure to meet you.' The consultant extended his hand to her.

'Dottore Marino. A pleasure to meet you, too.' She shook his hand and smiled politely, but

Orlando could feel a tiny tremor of fear running through her.

This was it.

And if the answer was no…

Please, don't let it be no. Don't let her hopes be smashed.

'Now, our friend Orlando here has given you a thorough medical. Everything's clear, and I expect you already know you've not been exposed to HIV, hepatitis or syphilis,' Gilberto told her.

'Of course I do.' She dragged in a breath. 'Dottore Marino, I'm going crazy here. I really need to know.' There was a note of desperation in her voice. 'Can we go ahead with the transplant? Please?'

Time slowed down to the point where every second seemed to take an hour.

And then Gilberto smiled. 'It's a good match. Yes.'

Eleanor clapped a hand to her mouth. 'Oh, thank God,' she said brokenly. 'Thank God.'

She wasn't sure if she was crying or shaking or laughing hysterically or if Vesuvius had just decided to erupt again: the world had gone mad.

For a moment she felt herself teetering on the edge of an abyss. And then Orlando's arms were wrapped tightly round her again and her face was buried in his shoulder.

'It's going to be all right, Eleanor,' he soothed, stroking her hair. 'Everything's going to be fine.'

She could feel his heart beating, strong and sure and steady, and gradually the trembling stopped. When Orlando guided her to a chair and sat next to her, she could see a wet patch on his shirt.

Just as well she hadn't been wearing make-up today.

Oh, lord. Last time she'd cried all over him, they'd...

She dragged in a breath. That wasn't going to happen again. Though Orlando kept one of her hands sandwiched between his, his thumb rubbing reassuringly against the back of her hand. Telling her without words that he was there for her.

Gilberto explained what was going to happen next. Eleanor couldn't follow much of what the consultant was saying, so Orlando translated for her. Though nothing seemed to stay in her head—the only thing she could think about was that the transplant would go ahead.

Bartolomeo had a much, much better chance of staying around.

And she would still have a family to belong to.

CHAPTER THIRTEEN

'DON'T you have surgery this morning?' Eleanor asked Orlando on Monday.

'Alessandro and Giacomo are splitting my list between them until I get there. I'm buying them *gelati* every day this week as a payback,' Orlando explained.

'Why aren't you doing your list yourself?'

He rolled his eyes. 'Why do you think, *tesoro*? I'm going with you to the hospital.'

'There's no need. I'll be fine.' She waved a dismissive hand. 'It's only an injection.'

'It's the first injection of granuloctye-colony stimulating factor,' Orlando said, folding his arms. 'You don't know how you're going to react to the G-CSF, so I'm taking you myself to make sure you're all right. Plus this is a huge thing you're doing. Even though you know what's going on, it's a lot to take in and you'd be struggling with it in your own language, let alone Italian. You need someone with you who can speak medical jargon *and* Italian. Which is what we agreed last week, yes?'

'Yes.'

'And that person is me.'

'Yes.' Though she was still feeling a little edgy with him. He'd held her close, comforted her, on several occasions over the weekend, and it was driving her crazy, being so close to him and yet *not* close to him at the same time, because he'd behaved with impeccable propriety rather than carrying her to his bed and making her forget the rest of the world. 'But you have your patients.'

'As I said, it's not a problem. Though if we could rearrange the rest of the injections this week for the gap between surgery and house calls, that would make my life a little easier,' he admitted.

'I can go to the hospital by myself.'

'You're perfectly capable of doing so, I agree,' Orlando said, 'but you're still not doing it. I said I'd support you, and I will.'

The first injection went without a hitch, though when the specialist started talking to her and asking her questions, Eleanor had to admit she was glad Orlando had insisted on coming with her, because for some reason her brain had turned to mush and she could barely string two words together in Italian. Orlando also managed to arrange her appointments to fit in with surgery hours.

By the middle of the week she was bone-achingly tired. Literally. She'd known in advance that she might feel some degree of bone pain because of the way the G-CSF worked on her body, but she'd bought some paracetamol from the local pharmacy to deal with it. Except it wasn't quite strong enough to deal with the pain.

'You look terrible,' Orlando said when he walked into Serafina's room after the Wednesday morning list, where Eleanor had elected to work in the baby clinic. 'Serafina, why didn't you tell me that Eleanor was feeling so ill?'

Serafina waved a dismissive hand at him. 'Because you would have made her go home and she would've sat brooding all day and getting miserable on her own. Which isn't a good thing.'

'And sitting here in pain is?' he asked scathingly.

'Everything's fine—isn't it, Ellie?' Serafina asked.

'Yup.'

But Eleanor's tone was too short to fool Orlando. 'You feel as bad as you look, don't you?' he asked gently. 'As if you need to sleep for a month. And you ache like hell.'

Yes. But if she admitted that, she knew he'd make her go back to his apartment. Right now she didn't want to be on her own. And she wasn't going to tell Orlando about the tingling either. She'd been given an anticoagulant to stop her blood clotting during the treatment, and she knew the tingling would stop shortly after she'd stopped having the G-CSF.

She lifted her chin. 'I'm not putting any of the patients at risk, if that's what you're worrying about. If I think my diagnosis or treatment skills aren't up to the job, I'll ask for help. I'm not that stupid.'

'Nobody's saying you are. But there's a limit to bravery. You're stopping for lunch right now,' Orlando said. 'And we'll see how you are tomorrow morning. If you're feeling any rougher than this, you're staying put. In bed.'

In bed. She wished he hadn't used that phrase. Because the idea of drifting off to sleep with him wrapped round her was more than appealing right now. And it made her want to cry. 'I won't be feeling rough,' she lied.

'If she's feeling under the weather, she can just sit in with me,' Serafina chipped in. 'Or with Chiara. I don't want Ellie to be on her own. She can't spend the mornings with Bartolomeo or he'll start worrying about her, and he needs to be as stress-free as possible for next week. She's better off here with us.'

'Hmm,' Orlando said, sounding completely unconvinced, and shepherded Eleanor out of the room.

The following morning, she was still feeling lousy, but not admitting to it. Orlando said nothing over breakfast, but he clearly guessed exactly how she was feeling. When they reached the surgery, he said, 'You're in with me today. Where I can keep an eye on you. And if I tell you to go into the staffroom and lie down for half an hour, you do it. Understood?'

She scowled. 'Stop bossing me about.'

'Those are the terms. Take them or go home. Your choice.'

She didn't have the energy to argue any more. 'OK. I'll stay here.'

She allowed Orlando to take the lead in all the cases that morning, until Paolo Barese walked in, complaining of chest pain. This was something she was used to dealing with.

'My call,' she said to Orlando. 'Signor Barese—'

'Paolo,' the middle-aged man insisted.

She smiled at him. 'Paolo. Tell me about the pain.'

'It's like someone pushing on my chest. It goes on for a few minutes, but it goes away if I sit down. I thought it was indigestion, but...' he grimaced '...the tablets don't make it go away.'

She had a fair idea what this was, but she needed to be sure. 'Do you get the pain often?' she asked.

'I've been getting it a couple of times a day. In the afternoons, mostly.'

'What are you doing when it happens?' she asked.

'Lifting furniture. I'm a carpenter,' he explained.

'Do you smoke at all?'

He looked rueful. 'Used to. My wife made me gave it up.'

Orlando already had the notes up on the computer and tilted the screen so she could see it. As she'd half suspected, she saw that Paolo's last blood-pressure measurement had been on the high side.

'Has anyone in your family ever had heart disease?' she asked gently.

'My father died of a heart attack in his fifties.' Paolo went white. 'Oh, *dio*. Am I going to die?'

'You're not having a heart attack,' she reassured him. 'I think you're suffering from something called angina. It happens when little lumps of fat called plaques build up on the lining inside the arteries leading to your heart. That makes the arteries narrow and not enough blood gets through to your heart—in turn, that means your heart doesn't get enough oxygen. That's what causes the pain—a bit like if you get a cramp in your leg, yes?'

He nodded.

'You might find you get the pain when you do something active, like moving furniture around or going up stairs,' she said.

'It can also happen if you're feeling stressed or angry, or if you've eaten a big meal,' Orlando added.

'Or even if you go out on a very cold day,' Eleanor finished. 'It's good that you've stopped smoking because that will help. I need to listen to your heart, if I may?'

Orlando was already holding out the stethoscope. She listened to Paolo's heart, the arteries in his neck and his lungs. 'No murmurs, no cardiac bruit and chest clear,' she told Orlando, who typed rapidly into the computer. 'It's all looking good so far, Paolo.'

His blood pressure wasn't so good—even if she made allowances for the fact that he was clearly worried, plus the 'white coat hypertension' patients tended to experience when an unfamiliar doctor took their blood pressure. 'We're going to need to start you on medication to keep this under control,' she said. His pulse was a little fast for her liking, too. 'Would you stand on the scales for me, please?'

Paolo patted his rotund stomach. 'You don't need to weigh me. I already know I need to lose a few pounds.'

'For your heart's sake, yes.'

'Am I going to have a heart attack?'

She wasn't going to lie to him. 'Hopefully not, but this is a warning that you need to look after yourself. You can carry on life as normal for the time being, but I'm going to send you to hospital for some tests.' She looked at Orlando. 'Which I'm sure Dottore de Luca can arrange for you.'

'I'll write the letters today,' Orlando said.

'I'm going to send you for an ECG—that's an electrocardiogram and it shows the activity of your heart on a graph,' she told Paolo. 'You'll also need a stress test—that's where you walk on a treadmill for ten minutes or as long as you can and you'll have some wires attached so the doctors can measure what your heart is doing, And you'll need an angiograph—that's where they give you a special kind of X-ray using dye to see your arteries, so they can see where there are any blockages.' She looked at Orlando. 'Start with diuretics for the blood pressure, yes?'

He nodded. 'And GTN.'

She turned to Paolo again. 'We're going to give you some tablets that you'll need to take every morning—water tablets, which will help reduce the pressure of your blood in your veins. And we're going to give you a spray called glyceryl trinitrate—GTN for short—that you can put under your tongue when you have any pain. It'll taste disgusting, but it will ease the pain.'

'But if it doesn't work or you need to use it more and more, you need to come back and see us,' Orlando warned. He printed off the prescriptions and signed them. 'The pharmacist should fill this for you while you wait. You'll get a letter from the hospital about the tests, and I'd like to see you again in a month to see how you're getting on. Chiara will make the appointment. If you need to come back before then, that's fine.'

'Thank you, *dottore, dottoressa.*' Paolo took the prescriptions, smiled at them both and left the room.

'I imagine you have a lot of chest pain cases in the emergency department,' Orlando said.

'And quite a few of them turn out to be angina rather than a full-blown MI. So yes, I'm used to spotting the signs,' she admitted.

'You handled that well—you did a fair bit of that in Italian, on your own,' he said.

'Because you've been coaching me.'

'We make a good team,' he said.

'That's not the first time you've said that.' She smiled wryly. 'It's just a pity that you're so obstinate.'

He frowned. 'How do you mean?'

'Think about it. If we can work as a team here, we can work as a team *outside* here.'

Orlando folded his arms, looking grim. 'We're in the middle of surgery. We have patients waiting. Now is *not* the time to discuss this, Eleanor.'

Yet again he was backing off. And she was sick of waiting. 'So when will you be ready to discuss it?'

'We've already agreed that. After the transplant.'

Give me strength, she thought. 'In the meantime, there's something you might like to think about.'

He frowned. 'What's that?'

'You,' she said quietly, 'are your own person. Your mother's given you half her genes, but even if you happen to look like her—and I have no idea, since you have nothing personal whatsoever in your flat—you're not her carbon copy. The way she reacts to things isn't necessarily the same way you react to things.'

Orlando rubbed his jaw. 'There's nothing

wrong with my apartment. It's perfectly comfortable. It's well furnished.'

'But it could belong to anyone. It looks like something an interior designer dreamed up.'

He spread his hands. 'And that's wrong *how*, precisely?'

Did he really not know?

And then she realised how neatly he'd side-stepped the issue she'd brought up. Distracted her into talking about his flat instead of the real problem—his conviction that he was like his mother. 'You're impossible.'

'Yeah, yeah. Let's see our next patient.' And before she could protest, he pressed the button to call in the next patient on the list.

Finally, on the following Tuesday, the stem cells were harvested. Four hours of being hooked up to a machine with a cannula in each arm, watching the blood flow out of one arm and into the separator before flowing back into her other arm. Orlando insisted on staying with Eleanor throughout the procedure. Holding her hand, the pressure firm enough to let her know she had his support but light enough not to hurt her.

This was more than just friendship. It had to be. He wouldn't be here for her like this if he didn't care. If he didn't feel the same way she did. If he didn't love her.

Would he?

That evening, Eleanor had to admit to an appalling headache.

'I guessed this would happen.' Orlando led her through to the dining room. 'It's one of the most likely side effects. Sit down and close your eyes.'

She frowned. 'Why?'

'Because it's easier to do this if you're sitting on a straight-backed chair.' He stood behind her, and she felt his fingers slide into her hair.

'Scalp massage?' she asked as his fingertips began to make tiny circles against her skin.

'Works well for headaches, because it increases the blood flow to your scalp. As does brushing your hair. Standard self-help advice for migraines, actually,' he said sagely. 'I should have thought to get some lavender scented oil. Massaged into your temples, it can help with headaches.'

'Hang on. You're a family doctor. And you're advocating alternative remedies?'

'Some of them are excellent. Aromatherapy's been used as a supportive treatment for cancer patients—the trial reports I've seen are positive—and I often refer patients to acupuncture for relief of chronic pain.' He laughed. 'Of course, some alternative treatments are quackery—pure superstition with no clinical evidence to back up the claims. But a patient's belief can do a lot of things. Look at all the studies on placebos.'

'True.' And this was making her feel good—the warmth of his hands, the firm yet gentle pressure against her skin.

She wanted more. Much more. She wanted to feel his hands stroking her bare skin. Teasing her, raising her desire to such a pitch that she forgot everything except his touch.

The only way it would happen would be if she begged him.

Even then he might say no. Might still want to keep his distance.

And her pride wouldn't let her risk that. Because how could she carry on staying here if he turned her down?

'Better?' he asked a couple of minutes later.

'Better,' she admitted.

'I'd prescribe paracetamol and an early night.' He fetched her the paracetamol and a glass of water and made sure she took them. Then, for a brief second, he touched the backs of his fingers to her cheek. 'Sleep well, *tesoro*,' he said softly.

She'd sleep a lot better if it was in his arms.

But she didn't want to risk him turning her down. 'Good night,' she said.

Orlando took the next day off so he could wait with Eleanor while Bartolomeo had the transplant. The plan was, he'd be there with her if she needed him and fade into the background if she didn't. And although the transplant went well and the earliest signs were positive, Eleanor's mood was bleak.

Over the next two weeks, while Bartolomeo was in hospital, her mood grew darker, though she kept up a bright, cheerful aspect when she visited her father in the afternoons. Visiting was restricted for the first couple of weeks, when Bartolomeo's immune system was at its lowest, because of the risk of picking up an infection, so Orlando waited for her outside the room in the evenings. But he noticed on the way home that she stopped smiling and barely spoke.

And one day he came home from work to find her crying, huddled on the sofa.

'Eleanor? What's wrong?' His heart felt as if it had stopped for a moment. No. Bartolomeo couldn't have gone downhill that fast. And she would've called him from the hospital, surely, told him what was happening?

Ice trickled down his spine when she didn't answer; she was clearly struggling to keep the tears back. 'Do you want me to call anyone?'

He could've kicked himself for asking such a stupid question. Of course not. She didn't have anyone any more—only Bartolomeo. Except... 'What about your friend, Tamsin? Do you want me to call her?'

'No. Ignore me.' She dragged in a breath. 'I'll be OK.'

He couldn't bear it, seeing her so upset. No way could he keep his distance from her—not when she needed him. He sat on the sofa next to her, then scooped her onto his lap and held her close. 'Tell me,' he said softly, cradling her. 'I'm here.'

'Seeing him in hospital…it reminds me of visiting my mum.' Her voice was so quiet he could barely hear the words, though he could feel her shuddering breaths, the way she was clearly trying not to break down completely. 'The chemo and the radiotherapy, and he's so sick— just like she was. I'm so scared, Orlando. I'm so scared he's going to die before I get the chance to know him properly. I'm so scared we're not going to get our time together.'

'Hey, he's doing well.'

'But what if he develops graft versus host disease?' She buried her face in his shoulder. 'As part of the transplant, he's got cells from my immune system. They'll see his cells as invaders and attack them.'

'Not necessarily. He doesn't have a rash, does he? Or jaundice? So your cells haven't attacked the tissues of his skin or his liver.'

'What about his gut? The nausea and the vomiting—'

'Are probably down to the chemo,' Orlando reminded her. 'It's not a sign that your cells are attacking his gut.'

'You know as well as I do there's a higher risk

of GVHD because of his age and because it's not a completely perfect match.'

'It's still a better match than an unrelated donor. And if he does develop GVHD, there are lots of things doctors can do nowadays. We can treat him with steroids, or an anti-thymocyte globulin, which will reduce the number of T-cells involved.' He stroked her face. 'And think of the other risks that increase the chances of developing GVHD—risks we can rule out immediately. One of the biggest is if the donor's had a transfusion, which you haven't. Or if the donor's been pregnant...'

His voice trailed off. Eleanor hadn't told him that much about Jeremy, and she certainly hadn't mentioned pregnancy. Had she carried another man's child?

The surge of jealousy was so powerful it shocked him.

'I've never been pregnant.'

And why that should make him so pleased...? He pushed his emotions aside. Now wasn't the time. 'So there you go. They're the two biggest risks and we can rule them out. It's going to be fine, Eleanor.'

'He had a sore mouth today.'

'Which happens with anyone who's had a transplant. And they find it painful to swallow at first.' He stroked her hair. 'And you know this perfectly well, but your brain's temporarily forgotten it because Bartolomeo is your father.'

'And I'm too close to the case.' She swallowed hard. 'He has mouthwashes. And tablets to stop the candida infection.'

'Exactly.'

'What about cytomegalovirus? Supposing he picked up CMV in hospital, and it turns to interstitial—'

'Pneumonitis?' Orlando finished wryly. '*Mia bella*, you're going to drive yourself crazy if you start thinking of every single complication, and every possible complication that leads off from that.'

'He's my father!' She lifted her chin and glared at him. 'I can't help worrying.'

'I know. But you know too much. And, as with any medic, you're focusing on the worst possible scenarios. Rare complications. This isn't good for your peace of mind.' He brushed his mouth against hers, intending it to be for comfort. But the first touch of her lips against his sent him up in flames, made him kiss her again. And again.

It was entirely mutual, because she was matching him kiss for kiss, touch for touch. And all his good intentions of waiting until Bartolomeo had recovered before sorting out what was happening between them went straight out of his head.

It was only when Eleanor had finished undoing his shirt and slid it from his shoulders and he was lying on the sofa with her on top of him that the tiniest, tiniest bit of common sense leaked back into his brain.

Just enough to make him stop.

He broke the kiss and gently manoeuvred them both into a sitting position. 'Eleanor.' He stroked her face, desperately wanting to kiss her again but knowing it was a bad idea. 'We can't do this.'

She dragged in a breath. 'Orlando…'

'We could give each other comfort, I admit. But we'll both regret it tomorrow.'

'You mean, *you'd* regret it.'

'I…' He exhaled sharply. 'Don't put words into my mouth. It's not the action I'd regret. It's the timing.'

'The time's never going to be right for you, is it?' She shook her head in exasperation. 'You're as bad as Jeremy.'

'No, I'm not.' The comment stung enough for him to say, 'I'm not sleeping with anyone else behind your back.'

She went white and stood up. 'That's low.'

He could see how much he'd hurt her and guilt flooded through him. He stood up, reached a hand towards her. 'I'm sorry. I didn't mean that. It wasn't my intention to open old wounds.'

She didn't take his hand. 'Your problem is, you don't know what you want.'

'I do. But I need time to get my head straight.'

'Time. It's always time with you. How much time do you want, Orlando?' She held up one hand, shaking her head. 'Don't answer that. Excuse me. I'm going to have an early night. Alone.'

And as she walked out of the room, the sun seemed to dim. He wanted her. How he wanted her. But supposing it all went wrong? Supposing he was like his mother, building up something in his head and finding that the real thing just didn't match up to it, and he ended up hurting Eleanor? It would be better to stop now than let her down.

Though there was this weird sensation in his chest. As if his heart—despite the fact he knew it was anatomically impossible—was splintering.

CHAPTER FOURTEEN

SOMEHOW, Eleanor got through the next week. And at last, when Bartolomeo was out of hospital and the preliminary tests showed that the new bone marrow was working—that he was starting to produce healthy blood cells—she knew everything was going to be all right. There was still a way to go, but the chances were loaded in Bartolomeo's favour.

Orlando was still being supportive, while keeping an emotional distance between them. And she'd begun to realise that, however much time she gave him, he was always going to need more. He couldn't learn to trust in love. Couldn't give them that chance.

Which left her two choices—stay in Italy and break her heart, or go back to England and break her heart.

So close to the choice her mother had made

thirty years before. To leave the man she loved—for both their sakes.

And although Eleanor was growing to love Bartolomeo, she didn't belong here. It was time to go home.

A few minutes later it was all done. Ian was expecting her back on early shift tomorrow. Her flight was booked back to London. An afternoon flight. Orlando would be on house calls in the early afternoon and then go straight back to the practice for late afternoon surgery, she knew. And because she'd chosen to spend the last couple of days with her father rather than at the practice, he wouldn't call at the apartment to check that she was all right.

Then it was the hard part. Saying goodbye to Bartolomeo. 'I have to go back to London. Back to work,' she said softly. 'I'm sorry I can't stay longer.'

'Eleanor. My new-found daughter. The one who gave me my life back—who gave me my hope back.' He held her close. 'I shall miss you so much.'

'I'll miss you, too. But I'll call you every day,' she promised. 'And I'll visit often. And when you're feeling up to it, you can come and stay with me. I can show you where I grew up.'

'And, if you would not mind, I can put flowers on your mother's grave. Flowers I wish I'd been able to give her while you were growing up.' He stroked her hair. 'Ring me when you get home. So I know you're safe.'

'I will.'

He brushed away the tears spilling down her cheek. 'Don't cry. This is *a presto*, not goodbye.'

To him, yes.

To Orlando… No. She couldn't think about that. Or she'd crumble completely.

'*Arrivederci.* And you do what the doctor tells you, OK?'

She went back to the flat. And then all she had to do was pick up her luggage, leave the letter propped up where Orlando would see it and get a taxi to the airport. She'd already made arrangements with the local chocolatier to deliver a large box of chocolates to the surgery, with a card she'd written to Serafina, Chiara, Alessandro and Giacomo to thank them for their hospitality.

At least Orlando's front door was on the type of latch you could lock without having to use the key. She'd left the keys in the envelope with the letter.

'I wish,' she said softly, 'that it could've been different. That you'd get into your stubborn skull that love really does exist—that we could've been happy together. But it's time I faced facts. It's not going to happen. I've given you time. Nothing's changed. So there's no point in waiting and hoping.'

She closed the door behind her, checked that it was locked firmly and headed for the airport.

Unease prickled down Orlando's spine as he unlocked the front door. He'd expected Eleanor to be back from her father's; he knew that Bartolomeo usually had a nap at this time of day. Yet the flat was silent.

Something didn't seem quite right. He couldn't put his finger on it: just that something was different. Something felt *missing*.

He found out what when he walked into the kitchen to make himself a cup of coffee and saw the envelope propped against the kettle. His name was written on the outside in Eleanor's handwriting.

A note?

Why on earth would she have left him a note?

He ripped open the envelope and scanned it swiftly. She'd written in English. Formally.

Dear Orlando,
Thank you for all your help during my stay in Italy. My father's well on the way to recovery now, so I am returning home to England.
I'm sorry I didn't say goodbye personally, but I think it's easier this way. For both of us.
I wish you a long and happy life.
Eleanor

He stared at the note in disbelief, reading it and trying to make the words sink in.

She'd left Italy?

She couldn't have gone. She just *couldn't*. He flung the door to her room open.

She'd stripped the bedclothes—knowing Eleanor, she'd probably put them in the washing machine—and all the surfaces were clean and bare.

The drawers were empty.

The wardrobe was empty.

All her things had gone from the bathroom.

Holding onto the end of the bed, Orlando sat

down heavily. She'd gone. And without her the apartment felt empty. Hollow. As if the centre had gone, leaving just a husk.

Without her...

And then it hit him. He couldn't be without her. Didn't want to be without her.

The One existed all right.

And he'd been stupid enough to drive her away. He might just as well have booked her flight himself.

'You stupid, stupid...' He cursed himself for being all kinds of fool, even as he picked up the phone and dialled the airport.

Please, God, don't let him be too late.

When he put the phone down again, his teeth were gritted so hard that they hurt. Eleanor's flight had left three hours ago. She'd be back in England by now. It would take her an hour, maybe two, to get home from the airport.

Except he had no idea where 'home' for Eleanor was. London was a huge place. And even if he called every single E. Forrest in the telephone directory, it wouldn't guarantee that he'd find her. She might be ex-directory. Or Eleanor might even be her middle name—so she wouldn't be listed under E. Forrest in the first place.

Stupidly, the one time he'd called her mobile phone, he hadn't stored the number. Chiara was on an efficiency drive, so a scribbled note from weeks ago would no longer exist. He had no way of contacting her.

There was only one person who could help him.

And this was something that definitely couldn't be done on the phone.

There was still enough rush-hour traffic left for it to be quicker to take public transport. And, oh, how slowly time could crawl. Orlando was almost beside himself by the time he reached the stop nearest to Bartolomeo's house.

'Orlando? I wasn't expecting to see you. Not now…' The old man's eyes glittered suspiciously. 'But I am glad. Tonight…I need company.'

Me, too, Orlando thought. Because I think we're both missing her like hell. 'I'll make us some coffee,' he said. *'Permesso?'*

'Sure.'

When Orlando returned with two mugs, Bartolomeo took one mouthful and gagged. 'What the hell did you put in this?' he asked.

Orlando spread his hands. 'Coffee.'

'About half a ton per cup,' Bartolomeo spluttered.

'*Mi dispiace.*' Orlando sighed. 'I'm…' He raked a hand through his hair. 'Hell. I can't think straight. Because she's gone.'

Bartolomeo frowned, as if suddenly realising something. 'Didn't you know she was going?'

'Not until I read the note she left me.' He took a sip of the coffee—probably the vilest he'd ever tasted. But it suited his mood. 'Do you have her phone number in England, please?'

Bartolomeo's frown deepened. 'Did you two have a fight? Because if she didn't choose to give you her number, I don't feel I can go against her wishes.'

Oh, brilliant. He'd just made things a hundred times worse. 'I didn't have a fight with her.' He rubbed his hand across his eyes. 'Look, I know it's not fair to ask you because you're still recuperating from the transplant and you should be protected from anything that might worry you. But I've just made the biggest mistake of my life and you're the only one I know who can help me fix it.'

'What sort of mistake?' Bartolomeo probed.

'I let Eleanor go back to London without telling her something important.' He sucked in a breath. 'I love your daughter. And, before you ask, yes—I can assure you my intentions towards her are honourable.'

Too late. Bartolomeo was already in defensive father mode. 'How honourable?'

'Marriage. *If* she'll have me,' Orlando said bleakly. 'I want to grow old with her, to have children with her—to wake up every day knowing the world's a better place because she's in my life.'

'That's how I felt about my Costanza,' Bartolomeo said softly. 'So I know how you're feeling right now. Knowing she's gone for good. So why didn't you tell Ellie you loved her before she left?' He tipped his head on one side. 'Or *did* you tell her, and that's why she went so quickly?'

Orlando shook his head. 'It's complicated. And I'm entirely to blame—it's not her. But I don't want to waste any more time. I need to find her. Talk to her. Tell her how I feel—tell her how stupid I've been to let her go.' Orlando propped his elbows on the table and rested his chin on his linked hands. 'I'm asking for your help. But if you choose not to, that's fine, too. Because I'm flying to England tonight, and if I have to visit every single hospital within a thirty-mile radius of Greater London to find her, then I'll do it.'

'If you catch a flight to London now...' Bartolomeo glanced at his watch.

Orlando did the same and realised what the older man meant. 'After I've gone back to my flat to pick up my passport, called for a taxi to the airport, taken a three-hour flight to England and then however long it takes to get to her, I'll be there at stupid o'clock. When she really won't appreciate a visitor.'

'Especially as she's back on duty tomorrow,' Bartolomeo said. 'She works in the emergency department at the Albert Memorial Hospital in Chelsea—you'll have to look up the address.'

'Thank you.' Orlando gave in to an impulse and hugged him.

'So does this mean you're bringing her back with you to Italy?'

'I don't know.' Orlando smiled wryly. 'I hope so. But if she'd rather stay in England, then I'll move there. I don't care where I live, as long as it's with her.' And, please, God, don't let him have left it too late.

It was raining in England. Which suited her mood perfectly, Eleanor thought. She'd called Bartolomeo from the airport to let him know she'd landed safely, and sent him a text when she got home, not wanting to disturb him in case he was resting.

How lonely the house felt. How empty. And even though she busied herself unpacking and opening windows to let the stuffy air out and cleaning the place until it shone, she was still lonely. Bone-deep lonely.

Orlando would have found her note by now. Ha. And what was she expecting him to do? Call her and beg her to change her mind? Hardly. Apart from the fact that she hadn't left him her number, he'd just take it as further proof that love was a myth.

It took Eleanor a long, long time before she fell asleep that night, and her eyes felt gritty the next morning.

And she nearly cried her eyes out when she

walked into the staffroom at work and there were banners everywhere saying, 'Welcome back, Ellie.' Cards. And a huge bunch of flowers from the whole ward.

'We missed you.' Sheena Redmond, the charge nurse, hugged her hard.

'Welcome back,' Ian said, ruffling her hair. 'Are you sure you're OK to work? I mean, you had a lot of travelling yesterday, and...'

She raised an eyebrow. 'And you've told everyone what I was doing in Italy?'

'No, but I got it out of him yesterday when he told us you were coming back,' Sheena said. 'You dope. You should've told us. One of us could've come out and—well—helped you recuperate.'

'It was a PBSC, so it wasn't invasive and I could've gone back to work within a day of the leukapheresis,' Eleanor said. 'I'm fine. And you know me—I'm happiest when I'm busy.'

'I'll remind you of that next time you haven't had a break for six hours and the patients are six deep in Reception,' Sheena said wryly. She hugged Eleanor again. 'It's good to have you back, Ellie.'

'Thanks.' She just about managed not to cry. At least she belonged *here*.

This was definitely one of the times when Orlando wished he was a multi-millionaire. Or knew one who had a private jet anyway. Even though this was the red-eye flight, the earliest one in the day from Naples to London, it wasn't soon enough for him.

At least he wouldn't have to wait at the other end. The only luggage he had with him was his passport, his wallet and his mobile phone, so he could go straight through customs.

Three hours. Three hours in which he hid behind a newspaper because he didn't feel like making polite conversation with the passenger in the seat next to him. Three hours to wait and fret and wonder if Eleanor would even agree to see him, let alone speak to him.

Customs didn't take long. Then he went for the fastest train he could get to London—and because he'd missed the last one by three minutes, he had twelve more minutes to wait before the next train, and then half an hour until he was in Victoria. And then the tube…

Finally he walked into the Albert Memorial hospital in Chelsea. Found the reception area for the emergency department. So near. Oh, please let her listen to him. Listen to what he had to say.

'May I see Dr Forrest, please?' he asked politely.

'Sorry, we can't guarantee a specific doctor. All our staff are highly trained and professional,' the receptionist told him.

'Perhaps I didn't make myself clear. I need to see Dr Eleanor Forrest, please.'

'I'm sorry, I can't guarantee a specific doctor,' the receptionist repeated. 'If you'd like to tell me your name so I can log you in to the system, a doctor will be with you as soon as possible.'

He didn't want a doctor. He wanted *Eleanor*. He was about to open his mouth to explain it was personal when one of the nursing staff came over.

Sheena Redmond, charge nurse, according to her badge.

'Is there a problem?' she asked, folding her arms and looking stern.

A woman who would brook no nonsense. He only hoped that she also had compassion. 'I'm not here to make trouble,' he said quietly. 'I just need to see Eleanor.'

'I'm afraid we can't guarantee you'll see—'

'A specific doctor,' he finished. 'Your receptionist told me. I'm not injured. It's personal.' He smiled wryly. 'Actually, it's good to know her friends here are looking out for her.'

Sheena's eyes narrowed. 'What do you mean, personal?'

'May I speak to you in private, please?' he asked, aware of the curious glance of the receptionist.

Sheena frowned, but led him into her office. 'Right. And this had better be good. Who are you?'

'My name is Orlando de Luca. I am a family doctor—what you would call a GP—in Italy.'

'Her father's doctor?'

He shook his head. 'I met Eleanor on the plane from London. We worked together when a fellow passenger had a heart attack. And I fell in love with her.' He took a deep breath. 'She's the love of my life. I was stupid enough not to tell her before she left Italy. And I need to tell her now.'

'Hmm. If you turn out to be another Jeremy—' Sheena warned.

'Hardly,' Orlando cut in gently. Then he grimaced. 'Oh, hell. When I left Naples, even the flower market wasn't open, let alone the shops.

And I was so focused on catching my flight, getting here to see her, I didn't— Look, is there somewhere in the hospital I can buy flowers? Chocolates? Anything?' He raked a hand through his hair. *'Porca miseria!* I have no English money either—I paid for my train ticket by credit card. And hospital shops don't take credit cards, do they?' He looked beseechingly at her. *'Dio.* The only thing I can offer her right now is an apology and my heart. And that's...' He shook his head in misery. 'That might not be enough.'

Sheena patted his shoulder. 'All right. Go into cubicle three and wait. I'll have a word with her. See if she wants to talk to you.'

'Next?' Eleanor asked when she'd finished writing up the set of notes and put them on the trolley for filing.

'Cubicle three,' Sheena directed. 'Fracture.'

'OK.' Eleanor smiled, and walked over to the cubicle. When she twitched the curtain back and saw who was sitting on the bed, panic flared through her and she grabbed the end of the bed to steady herself. 'Orlando? What are you doing here? Is it Bartolomeo? Is he all right?'

'He's fine,' Orlando reassured her.

She felt her eyes narrow. 'So why are you here?'

'For emergency treatment.'

She frowned. 'I'm not with you.'

'I require emergency treatment,' he said.

He had dark shadows under his eyes and looked a bit rough around the edges, but that was as far as it went. She couldn't see anything that looked like a fracture or a wound that needed dressing. 'For what, precisely?' she asked crisply.

'A broken heart.'

'A *what*?' She stared at him.

'And, as a doctor, I already know the cure,' he said softly. 'You.'

She shook her head. 'You're the man who doesn't believe in love. Who thinks it's all a myth.'

'And I was wrong. I admit it freely. It's not a myth. I love you, Eleanor.'

She wasn't sure she was hearing this. 'How did you get here?'

'I caught an early flight from Naples this morning.'

Her frown deepened. 'How did you know where to find me?'

'Bartolomeo told me where you worked. He

lost your mother—and I don't want that to happen to me. To us. I don't want to spend the rest of my life regretting that I didn't have the courage to tell you how I feel.' He raised a hand to forestall her protest. 'No, hear me out. The minute I walked into the apartment and realised you'd gone, it was as if someone had switched off the sun. And it was—oh, so *empty*. Without you, it wasn't my home any more, it was just a place to live. That's when I realised how wrong I've been.' He swallowed hard. 'So I came to find you. To tell you what's been under my nose since the minute I met you—what you told me and told me and told me but I was too stupid and stubborn to take in. That there is just one special person for me—and that's you. I want to spend the rest of my life with you.'

'You want to spend the rest of your life with me,' she echoed, looking stunned.

He coughed. 'I've been eating a fair bit of humble pie. Serafina has been having a fine time at my expense.'

Her eyes widened. 'Oh, lord—the surgery. Your patients!'

'They're being looked after by my very

capable partners. Who are also enjoying them-selves hugely, making me eat my words,' he said dryly. 'In fact, they made me say it several times, pretending they couldn't hear me. Serafina even suggested that I put it in writing.'

To his relief, a smile tugged at the corner of her mouth. So it amused her, too. Good. At least the idea of him loving her hadn't sent her scream-ing for cover. Maybe he had a chance. 'I want to be with you, Eleanor. I love you.'

'You love me.' She looked as if she didn't quite believe him.

Hardly surprising, in the circumstances. 'I admit I've been very stupid. I've made you wait and wait and wait. And I wouldn't blame you for telling me to get lost because I'm too late. But the minute I found your note and realised you'd walked out on me, it hit me. Without you, my life doesn't feel right. There's an empty space, like a black hole, right where my heart should be. Your letter…' He dragged in a breath. 'You said you wished me a long and happy life. Without you, it'll be long—every second will last a lifetime—but it won't be happy. Because, without you, the better part of me is missing. I love you.'

'You love me,' she repeated, still looking stunned.

'I love you,' he repeated. 'And I'm going to keep telling you that until you realise it's true.'

'How can I be sure?' she demanded. 'How do I know you're not going to change your mind and it's all going to end in tears?'

He smiled wryly. 'I think that was my line. Or it used to be, until I knew better. Because you taught me to believe.'

'Believe?' she echoed, frowning. 'Believe in what?'

'Believe in love. Believe in you. Believe in *us*.' He swallowed hard. 'You're right. I'm not my mother. I don't want you to change, to live up to some impossible ideal in my head—because you're already what I want. You're funny and you're clever and you're kind—and you're so damn sexy I have a hard time keeping my hands off you.'

'You managed it in your flat,' she pointed out.

'I was trying to be honourable.' He moistened his lower lip. 'Though if this means I need to make it up to you, we'd better go to a desert island for our honeymoon.'

'What honeymoon?'

'*Our* honeymoon. We're getting married.'

She coughed. 'I don't remember you asking me.'

He made a dismissive gesture with his hand. 'That's a tiny detail.'

'It's a big deal,' she corrected.

'Eleanor, I flew out from Naples at stupid o'clock when all the shops were closed. I've got no English money on me, so right at this second I can't give you a proposal with flowers and chocolates and a big sparkling diamond. If that's what you want, I'll meet you for lunch. I'll set up the champagne and the violin-player and the ring under a silver platter instead of your pudding. Whatever you want, I'll do it.' He looked at her. 'But right now, all I can give you is an apology. And my heart.'

'You're giving me your heart.'

'Yes. *Ti amo. Voglio passare il resto della mia vita con te.*'

'I love you,' she translated. 'I want to spend… the rest of my life?' At his nod, she continued, 'With you.'

He smiled. 'Good. I hoped you felt the same way.'

'I was transla—' She shook her head and sat on the bed next to him. 'You're impossible, Orlando. You've spent weeks keeping me at a distance. I've been so miserable about it. And now you're telling me you love me after all.'

'I do. It just took me time to get my head around it.'

'Time.' She rolled her eyes.

'I did warn you I needed time. And I could point out that you were the one who decided not to wait.'

'How much longer did you need, Orlando?'

He grimaced. 'I admit, you were right. It was when you *weren't* there that I realised what life would be like without you—what it *was* like without you. And I hated it. I want to be with you. I don't care whether it's here or Italy. The only place that feels home to me is where you are. So I'm telling you what I should have told you a long time ago. I love you, Eleanor Forrest.' It was time to take the risk. He slid off the bed and dropped to one knee. 'I meant what I said— in Italian as well as in English. I want to spend the rest of my life with you. Will you do me the honour of marrying me—being my love, my life, my one and only for the rest of my days?'

She didn't answer, and he felt himself freezing from the inside out.

He'd left it too late.

She wasn't going to give him the chance to make it up to her.

He was about to haul himself to his feet and leave when she spoke, her voice so soft that he could barely hear her. 'Are you saying, Orlando, that I am The One?'

'Yes. You were right. The One exists—and you are that person, for me.' His voice was equally soft. 'And this is a temporary proposal—until lunchtime, when I can do it with the flowers and the champagne and all the rest of it.'

'No.'

He'd thought it had hurt before. But this—this was as if his heart was being ground into the finest sand.

She wasn't going to marry him.

'Then I apologise, Dottoressa Forrest,' he said formally. 'I'll get out of your way.'

Before he could get up and leave, she took his hand. 'I meant no to the temporary proposal. Like you said, that stuff's just trappings. It doesn't last. Champagne goes flat, cut flowers wither, and diamonds…well, hit one in the right place with the right pressure and you'll fracture it.'

Hope began to flicker. 'So you'll marry me?'

'You're offering marriage. Which means… what?'

This was a test, he knew. The most important one of his life. If he failed, he wouldn't get another chance—because this was already his second chance. His *last* chance.

'It means a family,' he said carefully. 'Someone to belong to. You and me. And, in time, *bambini*—our children, who'll grow up secure and happy and knowing right from the start what I didn't… What you had to teach me. That love exists. That it's real. That it's good.'

'Then ask me again.' Her eyes glittered. '*Not* a temporary proposal.'

'I love you, Eleanor. My one and only. Will you marry me—make my life whole?'

She smiled and tugged him to his feet. 'Yes, I'll marry you, my one and only. And I'll love you for the rest of our days.'

MEDICAL™

—∿— *Large Print* —∿—

Titles for the next six months…

March

THE SINGLE DAD'S MARRIAGE WISH Carol Marinelli
THE PLAYBOY DOCTOR'S PROPOSAL   Alison Roberts
THE CONSULTANT'S SURPRISE CHILD   Joanna Neil
DR FERRERO'S BABY SECRET   Jennifer Taylor
THEIR VERY SPECIAL CHILD   Dianne Drake
THE SURGEON'S RUNAWAY BRIDE   Olivia Gates

April

THE ITALIAN COUNT'S BABY   Amy Andrews
THE NURSE HE'S BEEN WAITING FOR   Meredith Webber
HIS LONG-AWAITED BRIDE   Jessica Matthews
A WOMAN TO BELONG TO   Fiona Lowe
WEDDING AT PELICAN BEACH   Emily Forbes
DR CAMPBELL'S SECRET SON   Anne Fraser

May

THE MAGIC OF CHRISTMAS   Sarah Morgan
THEIR LOST-AND-FOUND FAMILY   Marion Lennox
CHRISTMAS BRIDE-TO-BE   Alison Roberts
HIS CHRISTMAS PROPOSAL   Lucy Clark
BABY: FOUND AT CHRISTMAS   Laura Iding
THE DOCTOR'S PREGNANCY BOMBSHELL   Janice Lynn

MILLS & BOON®
Pure reading pleasure

0208 LP 2P P1 Med

MEDICAL™

Large Print

June

CHRISTMAS EVE BABY — Caroline Anderson
LONG-LOST SON: BRAND-NEW FAMILY — Lilian Darcy
THEIR LITTLE CHRISTMAS MIRACLE — Jennifer Taylor
TWINS FOR A CHRISTMAS BRIDE — Josie Metcalfe
THE DOCTOR'S VERY SPECIAL CHRISTMAS — Kate Hardy
A PREGNANT NURSE'S CHRISTMAS WISH — Meredith Webber

July

THE ITALIAN'S NEW-YEAR MARRIAGE WISH — Sarah Morgan
THE DOCTOR'S LONGED-FOR FAMILY — Joanna Neil
THEIR SPECIAL-CARE BABY — Fiona McArthur
THEIR MIRACLE CHILD — Gill Sanderson
SINGLE DAD, NURSE BRIDE — Lynne Marshall
A FAMILY FOR THE CHILDREN'S DOCTOR — Dianne Drake

August

THE DOCTOR'S BRIDE BY SUNRISE — Josie Metcalfe
FOUND: A FATHER FOR HER CHILD — Amy Andrews
A SINGLE DAD AT HEATHERMERE — Abigail Gordon
HER VERY SPECIAL BABY — Lucy Clark
THE HEART SURGEON'S SECRET SON — Janice Lynn
THE SHEIKH SURGEON'S PROPOSAL — Olivia Gates

™ MILLS & BOON®
Pure reading pleasure

0208 LP 2P P2 Medical